A Break for Julie

Terry H. Watson

To Liz,

Best wishes,

Terry H Watson

x

D1744121

ALSO AVAILABLE BY TERRY H. WATSON

The Lucy Trilogy:

Call Mama

Scamper's Find

The Leci Legacy

Short Story Compilation:

A Tale or Two and a Few More

For Children:

The Clock That Lost Its Tick and Other Tales

Novella:

A Case for Julie

A Break for Julie

Terry H. Watson

Ramoan Press

Published in 2018 by Ramoan Press

ISBN Paperback: 978-1-9996502-2-3
Ebook: 978-1-9996502-3-0

A CIP catalogue copy of this book can be
found in the British Library.

Published with the help of Indie Authors World
indieauthorsworld.com

IndieAuthors
World

FOR JOHN AND ANNETTE

ACKNOWLEDGEMENTS

Sincere thanks to Kim and Sinclair Macleod from Indie Authors World for assistance with publication.

Thanks to inspirational Rebecca for friendship and encouragement.

To John and Drew for proofreading and finally to Christine McPherson for final edit.

In praise of *A Case for Julie*, the first book in *A Julie Sinclair Investigates* novella.

'Have you ever had a cake that was delicious, but you couldn't quite put your finger on which ingredients made it so? A Case for Julie is just such a confection. This novella is part Murder She Wrote *with just a pinch of a thriller thrown in and all stirred up with the exceptionally unique voice of this author.'*

Rebecca Forster, USA Today & Amazon bestselling author.

A Break for Julie is the second book in the series.

The door of Number 10 Downing Street, the prestigious address of Britain's Prime Minister, opened to allow an impressive-looking man to emerge into the London sunshine. A crowd of journalists and photographers surged forward like a sea of fiery white waves released from the ocean. They moved as one as far as the security barriers would allow and hollered like a horde of wild savages at Lord Smythe-Watkins. The man carried himself well: he had the bearing of one born into privilege; an aristocrat by birth and a gentleman by nature, one who commanded and received respect. *A Prime Minister in the making,* was the opinion of the political watchers. His full head of hair was well groomed, fair in colour, with a touch of grey where the sides met the firm line of his cheekbone. His dark suit was expensive, perfectly tailored, and sat on his solid frame like a well-fitted glove. From top to toe, he was every inch a man of importance. 'Sir, sir!' they called. A cacophony of questions followed, ricocheting across the space that separated those privileged to enter the hallowed building and those earning a living from stalking them.

'Sir. Lord Smythe-Watkins, can you tell us what is happening?'

'Sir, have you been offered a Cabinet post?'

The Right Honourable Jonathan Andrew Sinclair Smythe-Watkins, who much preferred to be addressed as Jonny, smiled, waved in acknowledgement to the scoop of journalists for whom he had the greatest of respect, and replied, 'No comment at the moment.' Then he was hustled into a waiting car that took off at speed to the Palace of Westminster where his life would take on a frenzy of activity. The short ride was not long enough for him to digest the enormity of his new position, and he arrived at his place of work breathless with excitement, his head mulling over a multitude of thoughts that raced around his brain as if a kaleidoscope with its fast-moving patterns and scenes had been released. He alighted from the government car and headed to his new office and a fresh chapter in his life.

The recent general election had turned the country on its head; people were insecure, concerned, and anxious about the future. They looked for stability from the newly-formed government, and the media were determined to pursue every avenue to report information, in their own descriptive and interpretive way, to the country ravaged by recent conflict, terror attacks, and economic hardship.

Settled in his office, with a generous splash of fine malt handed to him with congratulations from a senior aide, his first task was to call his wife with news that would both delight and dismay her. His call was answered immediately.

A long and anxious wait was over for the recipient, who grasped the phone with both hands, the instrument feeling like fire in her clenched and sweaty hands.

'Maggie, darling. I got it! My dream job. I've been invited to serve in the Cabinet as Secretary of State for Foreign and Commonwealth Affairs. The PM invited me to Number 10 this morning. I haven't come down to earth yet, I'm ecstatic. It's surreal.'

'Congratulations, darling. I'm so pleased for you. I knew you had your heart set on that post. Jonny, I'm delighted.

Do you want me to tell the children or do you wish to have that privilege?'

'I'd like to call them myself. God knows, I'm rather lax at talking to them. I'll call Robin when the time in California is suitable, and Leticia as soon as time permits this afternoon.'

'Remember, darling, that she is in Canada until the end of the month at a conference. You can catch her later.'

'How remiss of me to forget where my children are.' He laughed as he remembered the excitement in his daughter's voice when she had informed her parents that she had been asked to give a report at a Canadian conference for cancer specialists. Letitia worked as a researcher and, as part of a team, had recently made an important discovery that was to change the lives of so many cancer patients. 'The downside, Maggie,' he continued, 'is that we won't be able to fly to Australia on Friday. I'm distraught about that, as arrangements are in place and Hermione is so looking forward to spending time with us and showing us around the ranch. But I can't possibly be away from the House now. I know you will be disappointed, too.'

He sighed deeply, his emotions changing from elation to despondency within seconds. He nodded as he listened to his wife's assurance that they could arrange the visit at a future date, but he could detect the disappointment in her voice. She was the most placid of women, forever putting others' needs before her own, but Lady Margaret Smyth-Watkins was no pushover and held her own court when the occasion demanded. A childhood experience of bullying had seen her emerge a stronger woman, one to be reckoned with and whose gentle nature hid a steeliness of heart. This, however, was an occasion to be addressed carefully. 'Unless...' he mused, 'unless there was someone to take my place on the trip. Someone we could both trust to travel with you and to see to the package for Hermione.'

'At such short notice... who could do that for us?' Maggie replied as she perched on the arm of her chair, trying to keep the sadness from her voice while sharing her husband's delight at obtaining a longed-for promotion.

'Unless,' she said with a broad grin as if a light had been switched on, 'what about—'

Before she could finish, Jonny, catching her excitement, offered, 'Julie?'

'Yes, darling. I was thinking of Julie. Who could be more trustworthy than Julie? How exciting would that be for her? Although, I understand that she may have book commitments and events. You know how busy she is.'

'Let's ask her. Leave it with me. I'll call right now and get back to you. You are so right, my dear. Julie is the one person that I would entrust with my precious wife and Hermione's box.' Maggie replaced the receiver, sighed deeply, and thought how life would change for them. She was used to her husband's absences while Parliament was in session. He often stayed over in their London apartment, where she would join him occasionally for a theatre show when his schedule permitted, or when she wished to shop and meet with friends. The news of her husband's promotion filled her with some trepidation as she acknowledged that the job would probably involve more travel for the enthusiastic politician, and result in him spending less time at home. As an author, Maggie relished spending time at their country estate to indulge her passion, writing articles and short stories for magazines. No amount of persuasion from friends would entice her to branch out into writing a novel which they seemed to think was inside her, waiting to be written. She was content with her work, but there were times – especially with her children having flown the nest – that loneliness took hold of her normally contented soul. She sighed as she thought of how much more time she would have to herself and was resigned to spending many hours at her desk.

∞

Julie Sinclair's phone rang during a packed book-signing event. She ignored it and continued talking to people who had purchased her latest crime thriller and wished to discuss the book with her. This had been yet another successful event for the prolific writer. Previously she had published only historical fiction, but she had now found her niche in writing thrillers.

When her phone rang again, she switched it to silent mode and turned her attention to the woman who was interested in her latest book.

'I love your books so much, I can't wait for the next one,' gushed the woman. 'The characters are so lifelike, I feel I know them as my friends.'

Having finally reached the head of the queue, the woman had no intention of hurrying on and was happy to commandeer Julie's time and attention, despite the tut-tutting from others keen to talk to the popular writer. Julie smiled and thanked the woman who eventually moved on, leaving time for others anxious to have their book signed and to chat to the well-known author.

As she packed her few remaining books away, she felt her phone vibrate. She thanked the bookshop staff who had hosted the event and felt the phone vibrate in her bag once more before it went to voicemail.

Over coffee in a nearby bistro with her friend, Liz, who always accompanied her to such events, Julie finally checked her voicemail. She had one message from Jonny, their mutual friend Maggie's husband. 'Julie, Jonny here,' she heard him say. 'Can you give me a call back as soon as you get this?' Julie ended the message. 'Liz, I'd better take this call,' she told her friend as she sipped her one-shot latte. 'Jonny sounded harassed. I hope there is nothing wrong with Maggie.'

Maggie was the third member of the group who had met early in life while at school and had remained firm friends throughout their lives. Although those lives had taken very different paths, the women enjoyed a loyal friendship which saw them meet as often as time and commitments allowed.

'Let's hope everything is all right with them,' said Liz. 'Better call him now.'

Jonny picked up right away.

Still a little anxious, Julie said, 'Jonny, is everything okay with you folks? You sounded quite worried about something. Is Maggie ill?'

A breathless Jonny replied, 'No, nothing like that. Sorry if I scared you. It's just that I've been given a Cabinet post by the Prime Minister, which means that the planned trip to Australia is out of the question for me. I simply can't get away.'

'Oh, congratulations on the promotion.' Julie was genuinely delighted for him. 'I'm so pleased for you, but poor Maggie will be disappointed about the trip. I suppose there will be another opportunity to visit Oz. Surely, they will give you some time off. You can't be tied to those red boxes 24/7.'

Julie laughed as she waited for Jonny to get to the crux of his call, while mouthing to Liz, *Jonny's been given a Cabinet post.*

'Thanks, Julie. I wondered – well, we both wondered – would you be willing to take my place and go with Maggie to Australia? You know the purpose of the trip. All expenses paid, of course. Everything is booked, so it would just be a case of a name change on the tickets. It would mean a great deal to me. Hermione is so looking forward to seeing Maggie, and there's the question of the box of precious arte-facts for my sister.'

Jonny barely took a breath as he carried on, 'Maggie wouldn't be comfortable travelling alone with such a responsibility, nor would I be happy for her to travel on her own. So, you would be doing me – us – an enormous favour. The only thing is, the flight is booked for the end of the week, so it's not giving you much time. And I fully understand if you can't manage, what with your latest book hitting the shelves, and your book launch, and the hundred and one other things you authors get up to—' 'Jonny, stop chattering on!' Julie interrupted. 'Of course, I'll go! This is a chance of a lifetime. Hey, I'm almost packed! I just need to arrange for Liz, who happens to be sitting beside me, to take Curley. She says hi and congrats, by the way. I've finished my last book event for the foreseeable future, so nothing and no-one will stand in my way. E-mail the details with the arrangements about where and when to meet with Maggie.'

Jonny's relief was evident in his voice. 'Thanks, Julie, you are a friend indeed and you have put my mind at rest. I'm so grateful for this. Maggie thought you would jump at the chance but wasn't sure of your book commitments. I feel relieved now, thank you. I've arranged a two-night stop-over in Singapore, then Hermione will meet you at Sydney Airport and the three of you are booked for a short stay there with a city tour thrown in. It will help break the long journey and will give you all an opportunity to see places of interest and renew acquaintances.'

By the time they finished chatting, Liz, who had only heard a one-sided conversation, was intrigued to learn more.

'Sure, I'll take Curley,' she said when the call ended. 'I love that pooch but tell all. I'm intrigued.'

Julie related the news from Jonny. 'You know that Jonny got back most of the things that were stolen in the heist during his father's time as Lord of Chestermere Hall, don't you?'

'Yes,' Liz said, 'Maggie kept me in the loop about that. It was only right that the family heirlooms were returned to the rightful owner. The family deserve it after all the worry and the effect it had on the parents.'

'Jonny wanted to take his sister's share to her personally and had arranged the trip to Australia for that purpose. Now that he's been promoted to the Cabinet, though, he can't get time off. So, he has asked me to go with Maggie in his place... all expenses paid. I can't believe it! And stop-overs in Singapore and Sydney. It's surreal, Liz. I'm pinching myself.' Julie was beaming.

'That's wonderful news. You and Maggie will have a great time. Don't worry about Curley, he can live in the house with us. Our security is top-notch, as you know, but there's always a niggling worry when we turn in for the night that something awful will happen. I couldn't cope with another tragedy.'

Both women were silent as they remembered the dreadful incident some years before, when nine dogs Liz was caring for until they were rehomed, had been poisoned during her absence from her business premises. Julie's three dogs had also been boarding at the kennels at the time and had suffered the same fate. It had been a traumatic time for them both, and one that would forever linger in the back of their minds.

'It was all so unnecessary,' Liz said with a sadness that seldom left her when she recalled the horrific tragedy. 'I truly believe Bob Stevenson didn't mean to kill the dogs; he just overdid the poison. At least, that's what I'd like to believe.'

Liz was the wild one of the trio, according to Maggie and Julie. Her appearance was casual to the point of being bizarre, with her long, ginger-coloured, uncontrollable hair giving the impression of never having had a comb through it. She favoured floor-length skirts that trailed along the ground as she walked – or rather, bounced along. She looked as if she had come straight from the era of the 1960s flower power people. And the large pockets in her skirts were full of all kinds of doggy treats, keys, pieces of rubbish, and other unimaginable items that she often seemed surprised to discover.

'I don't think we will ever get over it, Liz,' Julie told her sadly, 'but life goes on, and you and Colin have done remarkably well in rebuilding *Safe Haven*. Curley will love being pampered. I seriously need to get him a playmate, I'll consider that when I get back from Oz.' She glanced at her wristwatch. 'I had best be getting off home, there's lots to do before the weekend.'

'That was an unexpected ending to a book event. A trip to Australia!' laughed Liz, as the two friends headed for home.

∞

The next few days were a frenzy of activity for Julie as she organised her packing, located her dog-eared passport from under a cupboard where it had entertained her play-ful pooch, and made several calls to inform friends of her impending trip.

As arranged, Julie met Jonny and Maggie at the airport. Both women were excited at the prospect of the trip – a first-time trip to Australia for both of them. They checked in under Jonny's supervision, having made sure that the precious package containing Hermione's share of the family heirlooms was safely screened with Maggie's carry-on luggage. They had requested a private screening to avoid scrutiny by other passengers and handed over an itemised list of the contents of the valuable consignment for perusal by security staff.

Following company policy, a senior security official was called to check the items. The name tag on his lapel read Reece Davies. He was an overweight, stocky-built man, his ruddy complexion showing evidence of an unfit, out-of-condition individual. He portrayed the air of one who relished power and, in his position of seniority, regularly exerted his authority among staff and customers. He believed his decisions were sacrosanct and attempted to impose this on Maggie as she handed over the box to be scrutinised.

Jonny and Julie were present in the room where Reece Davies checked the valuable cargo. They saw his eyes light up as he stared in awe at the artefacts and jewellery. Julie, who had an innate ability to read people, detected an air of jealousy, or was it more a case of resentment? She kept her thoughts to herself as she allowed Jonny to deal with the unpleasant officer.

'Ma'am,' Davies began in a confrontational tone, as he addressed Maggie, 'this box will have to go into the hold and not in the cabin, as it could be damaged in the overhead lockers. Passengers can be careless when they throw their belongings there.'

He expressed his opinion in an aggressive manner and expected Maggie to accept and agree with his words of wisdom without question. He was haughty and arrogant, and believed he was dealing with a lady who would accede to his demands.

Jonny was aware that Maggie was tapping her fingers on the table, a sign that his wife was becoming anxious and liable to kick off at the security man. He was also aware that time was moving on for their flight to board.

Addressing Reece Davies with the confidence of a man who knew his place in the world, Jonny pointed out that the box was more likely to be damaged when tossed around by baggage handlers or crushed on the conveyer belt. Or, worse still, lost in transit.

'We pride ourselves in this business of having total success when handling luggage,' Davies replied, still addressing his comments to Maggie. 'Your item will be safe with us, Ma'am.'

Jonny interrupted the flow of rhetoric from the pompous man and spoke with authority. 'According to statistics, Mr Davies, luggage in transit has more chance of being lost or damaged than that remaining with passengers. Six bags per thousand never arrive at their destination, and while that might seem a small number considering the amount of baggage that passes through airports, in my opinion, six in every thousand is six too many. My wife will carry this box with her on board. End of matter.'

The security officer, seeing that he had met his match in Jonny, huffed as he stamped the paperwork, and left the travellers to repack the box as he went off to photocopy the itemised list.

'Have a good trip, ladies,' he said as he walked away, his face red with annoyance, unused to his bullying tactics being challenged.

'Ignore him,' said a member of staff who came to escort them to the departure lounge. 'He's always like that, but his bark is worse than his bite. He likes to throw his weight around. We just ignore him.'

The women said a hurried goodbye to Jonny and headed to the departed lounge.

'What a dreadful man,' commented Julie. 'Jonny was a match for him, but how many passengers has that man bullied? I wouldn't like to work for him.'

'Let's forget him,' said Maggie as she marched ahead. 'We have an adventure ahead of us. Come on, girl.'

∞

While they relaxed in the executive lounge waiting for the flight to be called, they were oblivious to the buzz of airport activity: passengers queuing to check in; irate customers who had missed their flight; public announcements directing passengers to the correct departure gate; apologies for delays; swarms of people like energetic ants heading for a food supply; and the constant smell of aircraft fuel. The two friends had so much to talk about and could hardly contain their excitement when their flight was finally called.

They left the exclusive first-class lounge and boarded, promptly turning left on the aircraft, into the area assigned for those who valued and could afford luxurious travel. Both were amazed at the space allocated to them and the luxury of their seating arrangements.

'Wow!' breathed Julie, as she ran her hand over the luxurious seat. 'I never expected such opulence. I could get to like this way of life.'

'Me, too, I didn't expect this,' laughed Maggie. 'Jonny promised me luxury and a trip to remember, but, oh, he has surpassed himself with this.'

She placed her precious package by her feet rather than in the overhead storage area. 'I'll feel more content to have it here where we can keep an eye and my foot on it.' 'For such an unassuming man, Jonny certainly goes that extra mile,' said Julie, still in awe as she settled into a comfortable seat that would convert to a full-size bed as the flight progressed. She looked around the cabin. 'We have almost total privacy,' she remarked.

Their nearest fellow passenger was a gentleman who looked vaguely familiar. Julie nudged Maggie and asked, 'Who's that handsome guy over there? I recognise him from somewhere.'

Maggie kept her voice to a whisper. 'That's George Clooney, you idiot! Don't you ever watch television or go to the cinema?'

'Ah, so it is. Isn't he a bit of all right?'

Maggie laughed at her star-struck friend. 'I hope you're not going to spend the next twelve hours goggling at him like a love-struck teenager.'

They had barely settled when drinks were served, and they were given a menu to peruse.

'Where to start, that's a dilemma,' said Maggie as she pored over the extensive list. 'We can eat here in our seats, or in the dining area further back. What do you prefer?'

'Let's stay here for the meal,' said Julie, 'then we can explore later.'

'This is going to be some trip. Judging by this, we are going to arrive much heavier than when we set off,' laughed Maggie.

The flight left on time, and the two friends settled down to enjoy the splendour of their surroundings, whispering excitedly – not wanting to disturb their fellow passengers

– before eventually settling to sleep when night fell, and the cabin shades were lowered. Maggie rested her foot on the precious box, secure in the knowledge that no-one could move it without disturbing her.

When they disembarked at Singapore's Changi airport, the women took a little time to admire its grandeur before heading to the baggage reclaim area.

'I always worry that my luggage won't arrive,' said Maggie looking worried. 'That's why I wanted to keep this valuable box by my side. On one occasion, we flew to Basle and our cases ended up in Zürich. We were without them for two days, and since then I'm always anxious.'

After a short wait at the carousel to collect their luggage, the two friends headed outside to be met by a waiting taxi driver who introduced himself as Zhao Fei and greeted them with a cheerful hello.

'Z~ao, Niha~o, hello and good morning to you, ladies,' he bowed slightly. 'Leave the luggage to me. My cab is right here by the door.'

He led them to a clean, comfortable, and spacious vehicle, opened the door to them, and with a beaming smile loaded their luggage in the back. Maggie held the precious box on her lap, then sank back into the seat with a sigh of relief.

'I have a horror of something dreadful happening to this box before it is safely in Hermione's hands,' she confided quietly. 'It means the world to Jonny to share the items with her, and I won't fully relax until I hand it over.'

'Try not to worry, Maggie,' reassured her friend. 'So far, so good, and we have four eyes on it.'

∞

The twenty-minute taxi ride successfully switched their attention from Maggie's anxiety as the women gazed in awe at what the city had to offer. Their helpful driver pointed out various places of interest as he drove them to their hotel near the Shangri-La Orchard Road district. A delightful gentleman, his age was difficult to define as laughter lines around his eyes gave him a youthful, attractive appearance. He took great pride in telling his guests about himself.

'My family came originally from southern China, from Fujian province, a beautiful area. They came here to find a better way of life and blended in well with other nationalities. My wife is Malaysian, she is a cook in the university, just over there,' he said, as he pointed out an impressive building. 'She makes a great curry.' His smile was infectious.

'Oh, look at those shops, Maggie!' breathed Julie, her eyes shining. 'We are going to have some serious retail therapy here.'

When they pulled up outside the hotel, Zhao Fei announced their arrival then jumped out of his taxi and opened the door with a flourish. He carefully unloaded their luggage then took his leave of them. 'I don't feel right about not tipping that lovely man,' said Maggie. 'But Jonny gave me instructions not to do so. Seemingly, it's frowned upon, and banned at Changi Airport. It's seen as an insult.' She made a face. 'I've a whole list of do's and don'ts from Jonny.'

Once they had checked in, Maggie's precious box was quickly deposited in the hotel safe, with a receipt provided, showing the date and time of deposit.

'The item will be perfectly safe, Madam,' assured the smiling manager, who had appeared to welcome them personally. 'Your honourable husband has arranged with me for its safe passage. We pride ourselves in honesty here in Shangri-La. Enjoy your stay with us, and should you require anything, please do not hesitate to call.'

Rifki, as he introduced himself, was quite small, but what he lacked in stature, he made up for in a commanding presence. At the snap of his fingers, a young, oriental bell boy appeared and escorted the women to their penthouse suite.

'This way, ladies, follow me, please,' he said with the importance of a young man who took his work seriously.

The friends were thrilled as they took in the luxury offered by the hotel chosen by Jonny. 'Well, I'll be dammed if Jonny hasn't gone to a lot of trouble, with no expense spared,' exclaimed his wife, as she and Julie explored the lavish suite and admired the jaw-dropping view from their window. The two-bedrooms with ensuite bathroom included a jacuzzi hot tub, and the large lounge was furnished with every imaginable comfort.

After a brief rest from their long journey, Maggie and Julie explored what the hotel had to offer and made use of the luxurious spa and health suite before changing and heading down to the exquisite dining area.

'Where to start with this menu?' said Maggie, as she studied the *carte du jour.*

'I'm going to have some local food. When in Rome, as they say,' said Julie decisively. 'Let's ask the *maître d'* for his recommendation.'

A smiling waiter approached and bowed to them. He introduced himself as Haru, poured their drinks, and explained the various dishes. With his encouragement, they decided on *nasi padang* – a delicious Indonesian dish with rice and spices, which Haru informed them was a popular dish.

'That was scrumptious,' said Julie, as she pushed her empty plate to the side. 'I couldn't eat another morsel.'

Next morning, after a leisurely breakfast served in their room, the friends were directed by hotel staff to the nearest public transport stop where they purchased a Singapore tourist pass which allowed them to break their journey whenever they reached an interesting area of the city. 'Look how clean this bus is,' whispered Julie, 'there's not a bit of litter to be seen.'

'Yes, that's another thing on Jonny's list,' agreed Maggie. 'Don't eat or drink on the bus, and don't drop litter – it is frowned upon. No gum either.'

'I wish we had rules like that at home, or at least make sure the ones we already have are enforced,' sighed Julie, as she took in the sights of Singapore.

They alighted at the Orchard Park shopping area, where they were faced with the choice of two hundred shopping zones. 'Get me to these shops!' said Julie, amazed at the sight in front of her.

'Look at those dresses,' exclaimed Maggie, pointing to a display of exquisite clothes. 'Oops, I forgot,' she laughed, 'another of Jonny's helpful hints. Don't point. It's considered rude.'

'Hey, what about purchasing one of those long dresses as a gift for Liz,' Julie suggested, examining one of the colourful garments. 'It's the kind of thing she would wear, isn't it?'

Maggie nodded enthusiastically. 'Yes, she will love that, I'm sure. Let's buy it. Mind you,' she added, 'it will soon disintegrate, like everything else our wild friend wears!'

Their shopping day passed quickly and eventually the duo, laden with bags, returned to the hotel for a welcome pre-dinner drink.

'I hope we can fit these into our suitcases,' laughed Julie.

On their final day, the women toured the Botanic Gardens – a tropical garden of over one hundred years old. Maggie, a keen gardener, explained, 'This place was awarded UNESCO World Heritage Site, and well deserved, too. It's stunning! Just look at those plants over here.' She guided her friend over to view some exotic plants. 'This puts my little Village in Bloom Award in the shade,' replied Julie, who was a reluctant gardener and only made an effort when her home village was in the running for the annual award. She continued. 'If we hurry along, we might just have time to visit the National Gallery.'

'Yes, let's go there later,' replied Maggie, 'but there's no need to rush. It's open until midnight due to demand.'

'Another of Jonny's words of wisdom?' laughed Julie, as they made their way to the Downtown Core of Singapore.

'Of course,' said Maggie.

Their time in Singapore passed quickly, and soon the women found themselves back in the exquisite terminal of Changi Airport.

'It certainly deserves being ranked as the finest airport in the world,' commented Julie, looking around. 'Pity we don't have more time to browse around. Look at those shops, Maggie.'

There was little time to spare, and the announcer soon called passengers to board the aircraft for the eight-hour flight to Sydney. Once more, Maggie stored the precious box at her feet and sighed at the responsibility of caring for it.

'I'll be glad to hand this over to Hermione. I have a horror of something going wrong, even at this stage.'

'It won't be too long now until you'll be relieved of the box. And don't forget, there are two of us looking after it.'

∞

Julie settled herself in her seat for the next stage of the journey. 'Tell me about Jonny's sister,' she said. 'I know I met her briefly at your wedding, but that was years ago. What am I to expect?'

Maggie smiled. 'She's a sweet person, Julie, you will like her,' she replied. 'You might remember that she has similar features to Jonny, but while he is tall, she is dainty and quite petite. He takes his height and colouring from his father, but she is more similar, I believe, to their mother, whom I never knew. Despite her stature, though, she's a formidable woman and doesn't suffer fools gladly, as they say.

'Hermione went to Australia with some friends on a supposed gap year, after finishing university, and they lived on a ranch-type farm where people came for working holidays. Accommodation was cheap, and food was provided, but they had to take part in the running of the ranch. I believe it was quite hard work. It was run by Jett Lee who, with his father, owned and managed the place. Hermione fell head over heels in love with him and stayed on at the ranch when her friends returned home.'

Maggie paused briefly before continuing. 'Jonny's parents were furious, as they had mapped out her life for her. Well, her father really. They fully expected Hermione to return home to continue her law studies, but she became pregnant, married Jett who was much older than her and settled there. You might remember their son, Bradley, from the wedding. He was such a charming boy.

'Jonny said he will never forget his father's fury when she called to say she was married and that they were to be grandparents. Their mother cried for days, while his father apparently paced the room like a caged lion, saying things like, *how can she throw away her chances of a brilliant career in law for some common ranch hand that we know nothing about? What's his background? She has told us nothing about his family.'*

Maggie chuckled. 'Seemingly, his anger increased with every step he took, and he was like a raging bull goaded into action. *How can she do this to us, Bunty?* he asked his distressed wife, who could only sit and weep into her already sodden handkerchief. *How could she? I tell you now, that girl will not receive a penny in inheritance.* According to Jonny, he raged on until his anxious wife suggested he take a long walk around the estate to calm down. Jonny told me how he sat with his mother for hours that night until she retired for the evening, totally drained of emotion.'

'But it did work out for them, didn't it?' asked Julie, who was totally engrossed in the story.

'Thankfully, it did. Jett is a lovely man, older by several years but caring and loving to his wife and son. And Hermione loves the life out there.'

'I do remember him and Bradley at your wedding. Bradley was just a youngster then,' said Julie.

'Our wedding was the first time Hermione had been back since her father had cut off all communication with her and refused to take her calls or read her letters. Both parents went to their graves never having any contact with their daughter again.' Hermione shook her head sadly. 'Jonny kept in touch with her, though, and secretly showed his mother Hermione's letters and pictures of her grandson. But his father would not allow her name to be mentioned in his presence, and never knew that his grandson was a dead ringer for himself. It was a dark time for the family'.

'It sounds as if the elder Lord was a stubborn man,' said Julie.

'Yes. Jonny told me that once his mind was made up, nothing and no-one could get him to change it. Fortunately, I never met him, as he would have delved into my past and discovered my lowly upbringing on a remote Scottish island where my family crofted and worked the land. We would have been seen as peasants to him, especially as we spoke with a soft lilt, so unlike his cut-glass accent.'

Julie laughed. 'And you have held onto it, Maggie. It's a delight to hear your Highland accent coming through. I always loved to hear you read when we were at school; it was so different from the broad accents that the rest of us had. You have modulated your voice to fit in with your status in life, but the sweet lilt is a delight to hear. Don't ever change that!'

'Thank you, dear friend. Jonny says it was the first thing that attracted him to me. And there I was thinking it was my gorgeous, sexy body.'

They giggled and laughed like the schoolgirls they used to be as they reminisced about school days until they settled to a more serious conversation.

'I am so pleased that everything worked out for Hermione. Family estrangement,' said Julie, 'must be a most painful experience for all concerned. It must have been dreadful for Bunty – what a lovely name, by the way – never to set eyes on her daughter again. I'm sure there must be many dysfunctional families where some members are glad to escape for whatever reason, but for Hermione, who came from a loving family, it must have been a dreadful loss. And the stress for her mother must have been too awful to contemplate. Imagine not being able to have contact with the person you gave birth to. How sad.' Julie had just finished speaking when she gave a little laugh.

'What's amusing you?' Maggie was intrigued.

'Imagine me saying what I've just said! I totally forgot that I was adopted.'

Maggie, who knew the details of Julie's life, smiled. 'But that's wonderful. You feel totally at ease with who you are.' Her smile faded a little. 'I always felt sad for Hermione. Seemingly, they had been very close, father and daughter, and Hermione was the apple of her father's eye, as they say. Over the years, she wrote several letters home, but her father destroyed them without even opening them. Bunty, it seems, had no chance of collecting the mail as he had instructed the servants that all communications were to be brought to him, and him alone, regardless to whom it was addressed.'

She sighed before continuing. 'He was a bitter, arrogant man who only succeeded in making everyone else miserable. Poor Bunty. Her health suffered more from the stress, I believe, of living with such a thrawn man, rather than from the loss to her of her daughter and grandson.' She gave herself a gentle shake. 'Hey, let's get some sleep or we will arrive like washed-out rags.'

While Maggie donned her eyeshades and promptly fell asleep, Julie remained awake, pondering what she had learned of Hermione and wondering how she would get along with the woman who was to be her host for the next few weeks.

∞

Waiting in the main concourse of the airport was a rather weather-beaten but refined lady of short stature. The petite woman had to crane her neck to see past other people who were also awaiting the arrival of loved ones.

Hermione Lee could hardly conceal her excitement as she waited patiently for the doors to open and hundreds of passengers to emerge like a swarm of bees from their hive following their queen to form a new colony. She had arrived early and checked into the hotel chosen by her brother for the duration of their short stay, then changed into her town clothes, as she referred to her ensemble. Working on the cattle station did not afford much opportunity to wear anything other than functional, practical clothes, so she relished the opportunity to dress up.

Finding a gap in the crowds, she moved forward just in time to see her sister-in-law emerge from the departure area, beaming with joy as she spotted her in the crowd. Beside her was a tall, elegant woman.

'Julie!' exclaimed Hermione as she freed herself from Maggie's embrace. 'Welcome, welcome. I've longed to meet you again. We didn't have much time to get to know you at Jonny's wedding, but he and Maggie have told me so much about you. My brother holds you in high esteem after everything you did for us.'

She was referring to Julie's part in the recovery of the special items which had been stolen in a heist several years previously, and which were now in the precious box which Maggie was cradling carefully. Julie had played a major part in the recovery of the items and was a trusted member of the family.

With characteristic astuteness, Julie immediately warmed to Hermione. She was very like her brother, the warm smile enhancing her facial features showed her delight in the safe arrival of her guests.

Maggie showed the box to her sister-in-law. 'Here it is, at last, your share of the family heirlooms.'

'This is so exciting.' Hermione beamed. 'I can hardly wait to see what Jonny has sent over. Keep it with you, Maggie, until we're at the ranch. I've arranged for its safe storage in the hotel. I want to open it at the homestead with Jett and

Bradley. Let's head off to the hotel. We have so much to see, and I want to get to know this lovely Julie and see everything there is on offer in the Big Smoke.'

'Big Smoke?' said Julie and Maggie in unison.

'Ah, sorry! I'll need to remember to teach you our lingo. Big City.'

Their journey across town to the hotel took just twenty minutes. After the precious cargo was stored in the hotel safe, the trio wasted no time in heading out to explore what Sydney had to offer. Jonny, in his altruistic way, had organised a ticket deal which would afford them the best use of their stay.

∞

Their first port of call was to Sydney's iconic Opera House, where they joined a host of other visitors and were escorted around by a young guide – a student who was working his way through university.

'G'day,' he welcomed them all. 'Welcome to the tour of this impressive building. I'm Eric, your guide for the next hour and a half. This architectural masterpiece was begun in 1959 from an idea by a young Danish architect, Jorn Utzon. Have any of you heard of him?'

There was a murmur of replies: mmm, maybe, yeah.

'There's more information inside for those who want to know more about this ace guy. It was opened in 1973 at a cost of over a hundred million, way over the original estimate. It was awarded the status of UNESCO World Heritage Site in 2007, and I'm sure you all agree it was well deserved.'

Tall, with the build of an athlete and a charming smile, Eric led the group underneath the world-famous sails and onward through the building, pointing out areas of interest, answering questions, and generally making the tour a memorable one. He was informative, enthusiastic, and entertaining.

Architecture, he explained, was his passion. And after university, he hoped to follow his dream of designing an impressive building as Jorn Utzon had.

He continued leading his audience through the spectacular construction, through endless corridors leading to one thousand rooms. He pointed out theatres, halls, conference suites, and restaurants in the multi-venue performing centre, and his love for his job was evident. The tour ended with a genuine round of applause for the young man, and several people showed their appreciation in monetary terms.

'Thank you all. You've been an ace group,' he said. 'Over there you'll get some tucker and grog. Or here, in this direction, is Bennelong Point – the best area to eat.'

'That was spectacular,' said Julie as they wandered outside. 'I wouldn't have missed it for the world. What a charming young man. He had a great way of drawing everyone in and holding our attention.'

'Time to eat,' said Maggie. 'Right then, Hermione. You are the local person, so lead us to the best restaurant.'

'Ha! I'm not the expert in this kind of thing,' her sister-in-law laughed. 'Working 24/7 doesn't allow for much high living, and Jett and I seldom come to Sydney. In fact, the last time we were here was to celebrate our anniversary, and we were happy to go to a pub and have a counter lunch. We're not much into posh meals. But since this has been arranged by my darling brother, let's eat at Bennelong – the holy grail, they say, of Aussie's restaurants.'

She led the way to the chosen venue, where they settled for a pre-theatre meal. Admiring the décor, Maggie's eye was caught by one of the portraits on the wall. 'I wonder who he is?'

Their young waiter, hovering nearby, had overheard and asked if they would like some information about the eye-catching picture.

Handing over a glossy leaflet, he explained, 'He is Woollarawarre Bennelong, an Aboriginal whose hut was here on this site. He was what was called an interlocutor, a kind of go-between for his tribe Eora and the British early settlers, and he spoke on behalf of his people. The Brits gave the name Eora to the indigenous people around the area, right here, around the Sydney basin.'

'How fascinating,' said Hermione. 'I've lived in Aussie for most of my life, but never really took time to learn much of its history.'

The young man smiled, and said, 'I'll leave you ladies to read the rest of the information while I have the chef prepare your order.' As they waited, Hermione remarked, 'I'm more used to bush tucker. You two will sample plenty of that at the ranch. Jett's a good cook. We usually barbeque everything, you'll eat good Aussie snags, that's pork or sausage in a roll, and how about grilled kangaroo or witchetty grubs?'

'Mm, not too sure on that one,' replied Maggie with a rather serious look on her face.

'Kangaroo meat is low on fat and very tasty. You have to try it!' Hermione said. 'Oh, here comes our tucker, girls.'

They dined on a selection of dishes: grilled saucer scallops, followed by a suckling pig dish, and rounded the meal off with Anzac biscuits.

Wiping crumbs from her mouth, Hermione explained,' These biscuits are delicious. I believe they were first made by women to send to soldiers who were fighting in the First World War.' 'Mmm,' replied Julie, as she reached for another one. 'Very yummy indeed.'

They moved on to an evening musical performance on Sydney harbour, where they spent a delightful two hours enjoying the music, the atmosphere, and each other's company. The following two days passed in a whirl of activity that included a visit to the observation deck of Sydney Tower Eye, with its 360-degree view of the city.

The women linked arms as they wandered around the various tourist spots, each comfortable in the presence of the others, friendships firmly established.

With their time in Sydney over, they left for the next stage of their adventure. Julie and Maggie, clutching the box as if it were an extra limb, followed her sister-in-law through Sydney's Central Station to board a train for the three-hour journey to Bathurst.

∞

Hermione told them, 'Jonny asked my advice on this part of the journey. We could have taken an hour-long flight, but this way we get to see more of the countryside and get an opportunity to chinwag.'

'We are certainly good at that,' laughed Julie, as she settled herself to enjoy the journey. 'Tell us about your ranch. I'm curious about it.'

'We are right out in the outback. The journey from Bathurst will take about two hours, and Jett is meeting us there with the truck. It's quite comfortable really, although some of the roads are rough, but the scenery will make up for any discomfort and we have plenty of cushions and pillows! We head out towards the Gold Country – the site where the first gold rush took place way back in the 1850s when they used convicts as free labour to pan for gold.' Maggie interrupted, 'Did you and Jett ever pan for gold? Jonny often said that his sister was a gold-digger! He said it in fun, though. He liked to think you stayed on in Australia to make your fortune.'

Hermione laughed at the very thought. 'I wish! The only digging I get to do is on the ranch, for trenches or making holes for fence posts, but some of the early prospectors made their fortune around Bathurst. Jett's great-grandfather made a fortune from it; enough to buy the ranch that we live on. It's now owned jointly by Jett and Stan – that's Jett's ol' man – and his Uncle Barney. You'll get to meet them all. Jett is organising a welcome barbeque for you.'

She went on, 'Julie, to answer your enquiry about the ranch, it's a massive area – almost one hundred acres – and is a working ranch, with sheep and beef cattle. As well as our regular stockmen who muster them, we have a good turnover of visitors who come for farm-stay holidays, where they learn about cattle and go with the regulars to herd the cattle and sheep and ride the open spaces.

'This is where I come in. I run the farm-stay side of the business, the bookings and things like that, and look after the accommodation side. We have several cottages around the place, as well as bunkhouses. I supervise the meals and make sure there's plenty good home-made tucker for the blokes. There's lots to do, and we get to meet some inter-esting people. We usually have lots of students taking a gap year and want to experience life on a real Aussie homestead. Some of them stay in Oz and never go back home.'

'Just like you,' laughed Maggie.

'Yeah. I'll have to explain that to you both. Julie, you probably don't know about my evil past. I came out here on a gap year after graduation, before I was to take up a postgrad course in Law. Two friends from university were with me. I loved the life here – the wildness, the open spaces, and the freedom to be myself without the crushing restrictions from my father.'

She sighed before continuing. 'Girls, you must understand, my father was a most loving person. I was the apple of his eye, to coin a phrase, but he was a control freak. Every move I made was monitored, and he questioned everything: *Where are you going? Who are you meeting? Do I know their family? When will you be home?*

'I know that every parent asks those kinds of questions of their teenage children, but he was so in my face, even when I was well into my 20s. It was just claustrophobic, and I grew to resent him. He chose my university, my choice of course work, but I had no choice as he was paying for my education. I didn't even want to study law; it was boring. He checked my work assignments and, honestly, he was totally overpowering. I know he meant well, but he went about it the wrong way. I was awarded a good degree but there was no pleasure in it. I felt like I had been thoroughly manipulated.'

Maggie interrupted, 'I'm surprised, listening to what you've said, that he allowed you to travel to Australia.'

Hermione nodded. 'I thought he would never allow me to go. He more or less interviewed my friends' parents, and only relented when he discovered that an aunt of one of the girls lived in Sydney and we would be staying with her in our time off. Little did he, or we, know that there was no such free time available. We worked from dawn to dusk. I tell you girls, I loved the life and I still do.

'Jett ran the ranch and was kind to all us vacation workers, making sure we were well looked after. But his organisation of the household side of the business was a bit chaotic, so the three of us offered to see to the cleaning and cooking. He was grateful for our help, and so were the stockmen and visitors when we produced wholesome tucker and made sure the living quarters were up to an acceptable standard.'

Her pretty face broke into a smile as she explained, 'Things just snowballed, as they tend to do in life, and Jett and I fell for each other big time. He was a good bit older than me but neither of us bothered about that. By the time we were due to return home, I discovered I was pregnant. Jett was thrilled, as he'd thought he would never have a child of his own to take over the ranch. He proposed, and we were married on the ranch without too much fuss. His parents and Uncle Barney and several of the regular ranchers were there to witness the marriage.

'When I called my parents to give them the news, they were understandably shocked and angry. I spoke briefly to my mother, who was always the calm one in the family. She was concerned about my welfare and wept at the thought of never seeing me again, as she thought Australia sounded so out of reach, but I assured her that I was happy and planned to live in Australia. 'I remember saying, "Mother, it's not the end of the world. You and Father can visit whenever you like." But I knew deep down that my father would never allow her to visit. He was furious. He shouted and hollered at me, told me I was a fool and that I would never see a penny of his money – not that I wanted it; I had everything I needed. He slammed the phone down and I was left in no doubt that he meant every word he said.

'When Bradley was born, I felt euphoric. I'd never been so happy in my life, and I have no regrets about the choices I made. My only regret was not seeing my parents again. Jonny was my ally.' She paused to smile at Maggie. 'I would send letters and photographs to him which he shared with Mother so that she could see how happy I was and how her grandson was thriving. In hindsight, I think my mother had a difficult life with my father. He even banned me from coming home for her funeral. I went off to a quiet place and wept buckets for my loss – and for her loss, too, at never seeing her beautiful grandson.'

∞

The sad mood was immediately broken by the train conductor announcing their arrival in Bathurst, and the friends laughed and giggled as they made their way through the crowds all trying to alight from the train at the same time.

Maggie clutched the box even closer to her body as she made her way through the throng of travellers to meet Hermione's husband, Jett.

An imposing man – tall, rugged, and extremely handsome – he had long hair, streaked with shades of grey and tied in a ponytail, which enhanced his fine features. His eyes seemed to twinkle like bright stars in the night sky and gave him an air of a man at ease with himself and with his world.

'G'day, fair dinkum to meet you folks,' he said. 'Maggie, you look as elegant today as you were when I met you at your wedding. And Julie, I remember you from the wedding, as beautiful as ever. Welcome to Oz.'

Greetings over, they stored their luggage in the truck and settled down for the drive to the homestead. Maggie continued to clasp the precious box, never letting it out of her sight. As they travelled along – at times uncomfortably – Jett pointed out places of interest, throwing in some local history.

'This area here was originally occupied by Aboriginal people, the Wiradjuri people; they had their own language and laws. They have a strong presence around New South Wales here, and value their land and heritage and family ties.'

After more miles, they passed Mount Panorama racetrack.

'This here is an iconic racetrack, a landmark in the area, and when there are no races the public can drive around the track,' Jett explained. 'It's a public road as well as a race track. I took my boy Bradley there once. It was ripper. Ace. We had an exciting day.'

Hermione interrupted, 'And I knew nothing about it until Bradley came home full of tales of bravado.'

Jett laughed. 'Some things are best kept secret from the missus.'

Eventually, arriving at the ranch, they were greeted by four tail-wagging dogs. 'Here's your welcoming party,' laughed Hermione. 'Meet Patches, Kizzy, Benji, and Freddie.'

The excited animals wrapped themselves around their visitors. Julie, for one, was in her element as she fussed and petted them.

'These are our working dogs here on the ranch,' explained Jett. 'At the moment they are off-duty and love nothing better than meeting our visitors.'

'They are adorable,' said Julie. 'I'm looking forward to getting to know them and figuring out who's who. Patches is easily distinguished from the others. If they stood still enough, I might get to figure it out.' Julie laughed as she tried to entangle herself from the excited animals who knew they had found a new friend. Just then, a good-looking young man joined them. He was grinning from ear to ear with delight at renewing acquaintances with Maggie, and wrapped himself around his aunt, causing her to laugh as she implored him to let her breathe.

'Good to see you, Bradley. How you've grown! You were only a little lad when you came for my wedding and look at you now! Come and renew acquaintances with Julie.'

Julie smiled at the handsome man, who looked similar in features to pictures she had seen of his grandfather.

'G'day, ma'am. Welcome to our little ol' pad.'

'Oh, call me Julie, please! Ma'am makes me feel ancient. You were just a little lad when we met at the wedding.'

He laughed with the others as the mention of his last visit to the UK. 'I don't have much memory of it,' he admitted. 'I was fair worn out with the long journey, but I do remember the food. It was a feast to remember.'

Hermione laughed. 'A typical man, thinking only about his stomach, and not a word from him about how stunning the bride was or how handsome his uncle was.'

Brad grinned as he replied, 'Aunt Maggie. Julie. Allow me to introduce you to my wife,' he said, as he beckoned to a stunning, very pregnant, blonde woman. 'This is my darling wife, Milly.'

'You're married!' gasped Maggie. 'Hermione,' she whirled round to look at her sister-in-law, 'you didn't say a word about this.'

Bradley laughed. 'We decided to keep it a surprise for you. We've been together for twelve years, but circumstances changed now that the bump is on the way, so we did the decent thing and tied the knot here a month ago.'

Maggie kissed her nephew and new niece, offering congratulations to the beaming couple.

Milly, equal in height to Bradley, was blooming with the glow of pregnancy. Her skin looked shiny and smooth, and her hair glowed in the Australian sun that highlighted her golden tresses. Julie joined in the excitement with the newly-weds and added her congratulations as Hermione led her visitors into the main house where they were to stay with the family.

∞

The house was a traditional ranch-style farmhouse – a large, one-storey building, with a wide wrap-round veranda. The exterior walls were wooden, and large French doors opened onto a neat lawn, enclosed by a sturdy fence. The dogs, sensing that they were no longer the centre of attention, took off to chase each other around a nearby field, while the visitors were shown to identical rooms next door to each other, with a shared bathroom between them.

'Hermione, you have great taste; the décor is exquisite. You should have been an interior designer!' exclaimed her sister-in-law as she fingered the drapes and matching bedcovers. The light from the window lit up the room, highlighting the colours and catching the beauty of the furnishings.

'Strangely enough, that was my first choice of study when I applied for university but that was dismissed as nonsense by father,' Hermione said. 'I make all the drapes and bedcovers on the homestead. It keeps me busy, and I love making quilts from odd pieces of material. I enjoy working with fabrics, and art and craft... Talking of which, why don't we freshen up and get together over a drink and see what trinkets Jonny has sent over?'

An hour later, they sat around the kitchen table, which they were to learn was the hub of the house, and Maggie sighed with relief as she finally presented the precious box to her excited sister-in-law.

Jett and Brad, with a protective arm around Milly, gathered around to witness the grand opening of the container. Each item was carefully unwrapped and placed on a cloth, and Hermione gasped with approval as she lovingly handled each piece of her family heirlooms.

'Oh, these bring back memories!' She held up a cameo brooch. 'I have a memory of my mother wearing this when she was going to a black-tie event with Father.' Her eyes glistened with tears - of remembrance; of lost years; of pent-up emotions that she thought had long gone from her life. The others sat quietly, giving her time and space to open each and every treasure.

'Jett, take a dekko at this!' She unwrapped another exquisite cameo brooch.

He put his arm around his wife as he looked closer. 'Herm, these are ace! Beaut! We need to keep these safe. Do you plan to wear any of these?'

'I can't risk losing any and won't wear them during working time,' she admitted, 'so, my dear, you will just have to take me out to posh events then I can dress up and wear Mother's jewellery.'

Her husband laughed. 'The nearest you'll get to that will be tomorrow when we have the barbie for our visitors. So, I guess we need to lock these away.'

'I'm going to put this tiny painting by my dressing table and one or two miniatures, and the rest can be locked away,' Hermione decided. 'I'll bring them out from time to time and hold them to reconnect with my mother. They're so beautiful. Jonny made an ace choice in sending these to me.'

She clasped her sister-in-law's hand. 'Maggie, thank you for taking such good care of them on the journey. I love them! Brad, Milly, what do you think of your grandparents' treasures?'

'They are fair dinkum, but I can't see me wearing any of these!' laughed her son as he studied an expensive brooch before lovingly returning it to his mother.

'No, but someday maybe your cherished wife will wear them,' said his mother, as she hugged her son and Milly. It was clear that they had known Milly for several years and were delighted to see their son settle to married life.

'Oh, I'd be scared to wear any of these beauts. I'd be sure to break the clasp or something,' replied Milly, as she returned a precious item to Hermione.

Jett said, 'We need to take a picture of these for insurance purposes. I'll go get my camera.'

The cherished items were photographed and carefully rewrapped, returned to the secure box, wrapped in a hessian bag, then placed in the family safe.

Jett looked at Maggie and Julie who were fighting sleep.

'You two look rooted. Herm, we best let our guests rest. We have a big day ahead tomorrow – a tour of the station followed by my special Saturday night barbie. Go veg out, you two, and I'm mighty glad to have you with us.'

Both visitors had no trouble in sleeping, Julie's head hardly hit the pillow before she gave in to a deep sleep. Maggie's mind flicked like a slide show as one piece of the treasure collection after another filled her brain.

Eventually she, too, was in a profound sleep, oblivious to life around her in the busy homestead.

Next morning, sitting outside in the morning sunshine, they shared a hearty breakfast with some ranch workers who were about to go off on a full stomach to tackle the heavy workload. To the side of the main house was a large structure that served as a dining and barbeque area for the ranchers and visitors. It was set out with trestle tables and benches. From a nearby hatch, a cheerful Chinese gentleman by the name of Ju-long served breakfast to the hungry ranchers.

'Eat up, eat up, eat everything,' cajoled the delightful gentleman. 'you need eat Ju-long's good food. You eat, you all eat. Make Ju-long very happy.'

'They need food for fuel, that's for sure,' said Hermione, as she plied her guests with yet more mouth-watering items. We believe in serving an ace brekkie.'

The visitors were to discover that this was the norm.

'At this rate,' said Julie, 'we will be rolling home.'

∞

Jett, already up and about, collected the day's gear and loaded the truck before escorting the visitors to the vehicle that was to be their transport for the rest of the day.

'See you all later,' shouted Hermione as she waved them off. 'Don't let Jett make you work. Not on your first day, at least!'

Maggie and Julie, accompanied by four excited dogs, toured part of the vast station, leaving Hermione to see to the running of the farm-stay.

Jett explained, 'Ours is a working cattle ranch where we welcome tourists and visitors who want to experience life on the station. We aim to involve them in herding cattle, with some of our stockmen guiding them through the work in hand. Hey, there's some of them over there – Paddy and Bert, two of my best stockmen and good mates. Both are Irish and came over from the Emerald Isle on a month's holiday; that was four years ago. They are both dating Aussie girls, so I can't see them leaving here any time soon. G'day, you two, get your backs into it!'

The men waved back and continued working, showing some of the farm-stay people the trick of rounding up hundreds of herds of cattle.

'Hey, look,' continued their host. 'There's a few farm-stay folks who've been here a month now. They love it but they're due to go home next week. I'll take them to Bathurst for their train and pick up some students who are coming to experience our lifestyle. As I was saying, Hermione attends to the apartments and bunk houses, supervising the helpers, and making some good wholesome tucker. She's an ace cook is my gal!

'You'll sample her cooking at the big barbie tonight. We have one every Saturday night to end off a hard week. Only essential work is done on Sundays, to let folks rest up and veg out. It's hard physical work here, be warned, and some of the stockmen and the others can be a bit rowdy once they chill out and have a good bucketful of grog, but they need to unwind. Folks are harmless, but hell of a rowdy.'

He took in the two women's anxious looks and added, 'Don't worry, we keep an eye out for any sign of trouble and nip it in the bud. Hermione and Ju-long prepare the grub and I do the actual cooking; it's a marathon cook-in as everyone is invited. It's open to all the home-stay folk, and paid hands as well. It's something for folks to look forward to. As there's not much else in the way of entertainment out here, we make our own.'

Jett went on, 'You'll get to meet my parents – the oldies, Stan and Lilybud. They're looking forward to you Pommies, with the greatest respect, coming along tonight to talk about the dear old UK, and you'll get to meet my Uncle Barney.

He's too infirm now to do any ranch work but enjoys being taken out with the blokes and watching them work. We might lob in to see him; we'll be passing his place later.'

He pointed to a group of people who were busy erecting fence posts. 'See that squad over there? That's the latest bunch of trainee hands – Jackaroos, we call them; and the girls, well, they're Jillaroos. Some have come from college to do practical work with us and make a dollar or two. Hey, there's Uncle Barney, he must have come for the ride with some of the guys. We'll call over and have a bite to eat with him. Hermione has packed enough to feed us all.'

Julie and Maggie were glad to get down from the vehicle and stretch their legs, and the excited dogs were happy to join them.

Barney grinned at the two women as he was introduced, showing an almost toothless smile. He had one fang that wobbled as he spoke. He was a delightful man who, despite a serious illness some years before, entertained the visitors with his wit and wisdom.

'Now, Uncle Barney, don't you go filling these gals' heads full of your nonsense,' laughed Jett, as he handed round the sandwiches to all and sundry. 'Have a sanger, ladies, we've got cheese, eggs, kangaroo meat, and lots of other fillings, and plenty of the missus's baking. Bog in.'

Despite having eaten a large breakfast, Julie realised she was really hungry. She and Maggie were captivated by the old man's tales of his life on the ranch.

At one point, Maggie turned to her and said, 'There's a story there somewhere, Julie!'

She nodded. 'That had crossed my mind too! Hmm, something to think about.'

Uncle Barney loved nothing more than a captive audience, and Jett groaned as his uncle regaled the visitors with a tale of bravado which had grown arms and legs with each telling.

'It happened one Sunday when I took my old gal, my darling Maddie, for a stroll around the homestead. Maddie by name and mad by nature,' he laughed at his own telling of the tale. 'Well, as I was saying, it was getting dark. Not proper dark like, just a tad darker than it had been a few hours earlier. Now my Maddie, the love of my life... did I tell you gals she passed away some ten years ago? Miss her more each day.' He wiped a tear from the corner of his eye. 'Well, this particular Saturday—'

'Sunday, you old scoundrel!' interrupted Jett.

'Whose story is this, young whippersnapper? Young uns today, ladies, they have no manners... As I was saying, it got kinda dark and my Maddie, she didn't much like the dark, so I put my arm around her... Did I say we wasn't married, just kinda courting? So, there we were. We sat on a rock and, well, you know how it is, we got a bit friendly like, then she screamed her head off. I pulled away thinking I must have offended her like, but she pointed to the bottom of the rock and there was the biggest, most poisonous snake known to man heading for her leg... Well, me being the chivalrous kind, fended it off. It tried to fight me, its ferocious fangs aiming for my arm, but it was no match for Barney-Boy here. I killed it stone ginger and became a hero to my Maddie... Then—'

'Uncle Barney,' Jett interrupted gently. 'As riveting as your story is, I have to get our guests moving on, so say your fare-wells until you meet up tonight as the barbeque. We've a lot to see yet.'

With a smile and a bow from the waist, Barney took his leave of the visitors and toddled over to join the Jillaroos to help, or hinder them, as was his delightful way.

'He's a fascinating old fellow,' exclaimed Julie as she boarded the Jeep for the next part of the tour.

'He likes nothing better than telling a tale or two to a captive audience. I'm sure that snake was a harmless adder, if it ever existed at all,' laughed Jett, as he drove off with a wave of the hand.

They moved on to explore more of the ranch, waving when prompted by their host. 'See you all tonight at the barbie,' he called to the various groups. 'Do you gals ride?' he asked. 'We have some great stock horses here, calm beasts with good temperament. They are our main work horses. If you want to ride out while you're here I'll arrange for Smokey to guide you... he's an ace rider and his main work here, apart from looking after the horses, is to take visitors for lessons, many of whom have never ridden. So, if you fancy a few lessons, I'll introduce Smokey tonight at the barbie. We call him Smokey for obvious reasons, his real name is Harry.'

'I used to ride,' replied Maggie. 'It's been a while, but I'm up for a refresher session.'

'I'm game,' said Julie, 'although I've never ridden anything other than my bike, but I'll give it a go.'

'We also have quad bikes that the stockmen use to cover the miles of terrain. We'll take you for a spin if you feel brave enough.' Jett laughed at the expression on Maggie's face.

After an exhilarating day, they returned to the homestead to rest a while, out of the searing heat of the Australian sun.

'It'll be a tad cooler this evening in the barbie marquee,' Jett assured them. 'The only heat will come from sweaty bodies when the dancing takes over the footless and left-footed ranch-guys.'

∞

The barbeque was a spectacular event. Hermione and Ju-long had prepared mountains of food for Jett to cook on the massive barbeque. The smell drew everyone from the station to gather in anticipation of what promised to be an eventful evening. Introductions were made and Julie, who was always interested in meeting new people, found it difficult to keep track of who was who.

She tucked into one of Jett's special Aussie snags as she walked around chatting to ranch hands and farm-stay visitors. Jett caught her eye and waved her over to where an elderly couple sat enjoying their tucker.

'Hey, Julie, come and meet the oldies! Julie, meet my parents, Stan and Lilybud. They are dying to meet a real Pommie writer!' 'G'day, ma'am. Welcome to the outback. It's sure nice to meet you,' said an elderly version of Jett. The man hadn't lost any of his charm, and his twinkling eyes shone from a well-worn, weather-beaten face. As he stood to greet Julie, he rose to his full height. He was ramrod straight, the only sign of ageing his use of a walking cane which he held in front of him, both hands on the carved wooden handle that depicted a kangaroo.

'Carved it myself,' he said, as he noticed Julie's eyes on it. 'It's served me well, has the old Roo. Made it myself from a piece of driftwood many years ago.'

'It's a beautiful cane, so sturdy, too,' replied Julie.

Lilybud, less agile than her husband, remained seated as the introductions were made. She smiled and grasped Julie's hands in hers.

'Welcome to Oz, we're so happy to meet you.' She leant over and whispered in her ear, 'I've read some of your books. Hermione arranged with Maggie to get them for me. Tell me,' she continued, as she drew closer to the writer, 'was that character Zac really the killer? He seemed such a nice man.'

Julie laughed as she sat beside the delightful woman to discuss the ins and outs of her characters.

Before long, music started up from an impromptu band. One of the stockmen of Aboriginal descent played a long, droning sound to call the musicians together and to announce the start of musical festivities. Neither Maggie nor Julie had heard a didgeridoo being played and were fascinated by the instrument. They spoke with Kwame, who described the instrument to them.

'This belonged to my grandfather, who fashioned it himself from a branch of a eucalyptus tree and used it mainly in ceremonials and as a call to meditate. Nowadays, I use it at Jett's barbie to call people together to feast and relax.' He laughed as he continued, 'Once the grog gets going and dancing starts, it can get a bit wild. The blokes work hard, and this is a form of relaxation for them.'

Julie reverently studied the instrument and, to Kwame's amusement, attempted to emit a sound... to no avail.

'It's a hard instrument to play,' she said, 'I admire your skill, Kwame.'

Maggie declined the offer to try. 'I don't have enough puff to blow that,' she laughed. 'Tell me, Kwame, where does your name come from?'

He smiled as he replied, 'It means born on Saturday.'

'Oh,' said Maggie, 'my son was born on Saturday. Now I'll have to call him Kwame Robin!'

He put the instrument to his lips and emitted a deep, throaty note and within minutes the party goers began gathering around the main area where Jett and Hermione stood together, ready to declare the party open. This was a ritual that began every barbeque, apparently, and gave Jett an opportunity to make announcements to the crowd.

'This evening,' he began, 'is special for two reasons. We are honoured to welcome some Pommies to our homestead. Maggie is married to Hermione's brother, and her friend Julie, who accompanied her, is a writer of great esteem. Welcome, ladies, welcome.'

Once the applause had died down, Jett once more called for attention. 'Some of you who know our son Bradley, are aware that he and Milly were married here some weeks ago. We kept the celebrations until now, to share the joy with Maggie and Julie. So, guys and gals, Jackaroos, Jillaroos, all of you, lift your glasses, jugs, tankers, whatever you have, and join in a toast to Bradley and Milly.'

Bradley and Milly, chorused the crowd. *Bradley and Milly,* they called.

Bradley took his wife's arm and whirled her carefully around the assembled crowd to acknowledge their wishes.

'Thank you all, thank you,' he called.

The festivities continued with an endless supply of food and drink being consumed. Julie found herself being whirled around the dance area as Maggie, sitting now with Jett's parents, laughed and clapped in time to the music. She was spotted by one of the Jackaroos, who literally lifted her off her feet, spun her around, and danced a quick barn dance with the giggling visitor. As the night progressed, laughter became louder and raucous, with more and more drink consumed.

'These guys certainly know how to party,' giggled Maggie, who couldn't remember when she last had such fun. She caught up with her nephew and sat chatting to him despite the noise going on around them.

'Milly and I met at university,' explained Bradley. 'I was studying agriculture and Milly was doing business studies. We bumped into each other, quite literally, in the coffee bar when I stepped back, and she spilled her drink. I apologised and offered to buy her a replacement. We sat together and chatted for so long that we both missed our lecture. We seemed to click almost from that incident. It turned out that neither of us were enjoying our studies, and I had already spoken to my ol' man about leaving uni and working full time at the homestead.'

He went on, 'I knew more about ranching than some of my lecturers, and Milly was bored out of her mind with her course. She had previously worked with a firm of account-ants and had picked up enough knowledge and skills to go it alone. We needed accountancy help here, so, to cut a long story short, we gave up uni and started working together. We hated being apart from each other and the oldies, bless 'em, agreed that we could move into one of the cottages. When Milly fell pregnant, we decided to tie the knot. Aunt Maggie, I've never been happier in my life, and sure am pleased that you are here to share my happiness.'

They talked some more until the noise level made it almost impossible for them to communicate without shouting. When Julie joined them, the young man excused himself to check on Milly who was attempting to rest.

'Sorry about the noise level,' he told the two women, 'it will get worse as the night goes on. I best go and check that she's okay. I might as well turn in for the night.'

'Yes, we were warned that it would be a bit on the wild side,' laughed Julie. 'I've enjoyed the evening. It has blown the cobwebs away, and to think that we will have this each Saturday while we are here! I'm off to retire for the night, too. I can't take much more frivolity.' And she staggered off to the main house, and bed.

∞

The following day, being Sunday, was a quiet, subdued day to allow guests and workforce to rest up and, for many, to sleep off the effects of the previous evening's festivities. Julie sat outside with Maggie and Hermione, chatting about life in general and the people they had met the previous evening.

Hermione asked her guests, 'Are you ready for riding tomorrow? I believe Smokey will call over after breakfast and collect his pupils.'

'I'm looking forward to a refresher course,' replied Maggie. 'It's a while since I've sat on a saddle.'

'It will be a first for me,' said Julie. 'I'm hoping the horse and I are compatible.'

Hermione assured her, 'Smokey has everything organised. He's an ace rider and very patient. You'll have no problem, believe me.'

∞

In the early hours of the night, Julie awoke with a dreadful headache and rushed to the bathroom where she was violently sick. Maggie, alerted by the noise, came through from her room to assist her.

'Julie, you look dreadful. Let me help you get back to bed.'

Julie held onto her friend as the room seemed to swim around. She found it hard to focus and flopped into bed, holding her head in her hands.

'I think you're having a migraine attack, my dear,' said Maggie gently as she tucked Julie in. 'Have you had this kind of thing before?'

Julie managed to mumble, 'Once, many years ago. I feel ghastly. I just want to curl up and sleep.'

'I'll put the light out, as that can irritate things. I'll be next door with my door open. Call out if you need me. What you need most of all is sleep.'

Julie nodded and mumbled her thanks as she pulled the covers over her head and attempted to sleep. Her head throbbed as if minions were jumping on it and playing with drumsticks. Every time she tried to move, the room seemed to swirl around her; she had never felt so ill in her life.

Maggie had left some painkillers, but the very act of lifting the glass of water had her screaming in agony and brought a concerned Hermione and Maggie rushing to her bedside.

'Here, let me help you,' said Hermione as she gently lifted the water to Julie's lips. 'These painkillers should knock you out for a while. You need to shade your eyes from the light.'

Maggie closed over the heavy curtains and produced a sleep mask. 'Fortunately, I rescued this from the plane journey. Put this on and try to sleep.'

'There will be no riding for you today,' said her hostess.

Julie tried to smile at the remark, but even that hurt.

'Don't worry. I'll be here all day working on paperwork,' said Hermione. 'I'll look after you.'

Her friends were understandably concerned about Julie's condition. 'The nearest hospital is at Bathurst, should we need it, but I'm sure she'll recover in the next few days,' Hermione told Maggie. 'We need to keep her off triggers like caffeine and red wine. You go off with Smokey for your ride. I'll be here for Julie. If she doesn't show signs of improvement, we'll have someone drive over to Bathurst to bring a doc back, and if she worsens, we can call on the flying doctor service. They offer 24-hour emergency care.'

Seeing the concern on Maggie's face, Hermione assured her that all would be well. 'I've experienced people with migraine attacks,' she said, 'so please don't worry. Go! Enjoy your ride with Smokey and Dandy Boy. He's a fine horse with a good nature.'

∞

After breakfast, and geared up and ready to go, Maggie was introduced to her horse.

'Here he is, your ride for the day, Dandy Boy,' said Smokey. 'One of the most placid of our stock horses. Sorry to hear your mate is ill.' Maggie fussed over her new friend before being hoisted up on to the saddle. Smokey, an affable bloke, was one of the station's farriers, whose work earned him the name of Smokey as he spent hours toiling over hot coals. Dirt on his face looked ingrained, and when he smiled it made a spider effect of different colours that added to his attraction. He guided Maggie through the basics before issuing the 'walk on' signal.

'The plan,' he said as they rode along – he on his favourite stead Windsor, Maggie comfortable on Dandy Boy – 'since this is your first ride, is that we'll take the easy path to Wild Creek and see some spectacular views, then circle back onto a route that will take us home via one of the drover stations where some of the stockmen live in bunkhouses. All in all, it's about twenty clicks. That's kilometres to you. That should be enough for a first ride.'

Maggie, comfortable in the saddle and with complete faith in her guide, relaxed and enjoyed the scenery as it unfolded before her, while exchanging stories with her affable tutor about her country estate, her political husband, and her amazing family.

'Everyone thinks their children are wonderful, and I certainly do,' she continued, as she related stories of their individual achievements while Smokey listened intently. She had temporarily forgotten about Julie's plight.

'Your youngsters sound ace kids, no wonder you are proud of them,' he said. 'And to have such a clever husband, you have a right to be a proud mama. I never had much time for politics myself but listening to you about your man could change my views. I might just take more interest, and I'll be looking out for his name in the papers. We get UK news here regularly.'

The miles, or clicks as Smokey referred to them, seemed to fly by with Maggie feeling like an accomplished rider.

'They say that once you learn to ride a bike, you never forget the skill. It must be the same with riding,' she joked. 'I feel I've been doing this all my life.'

'Ma'am, you sure are ace – one of the best riders I've taken out for some time. Right, here we are at Wild Creek. We'll give the horses a rest and tuck into the sangers that Hermione packed for us. She sure knows how to feed folks.'

∞

At the ranch, Julie, rallying slightly, lifted her head when she heard someone in the kitchen area which was near her bedroom. Hermione had left the door ajar.

'Who's there?' she called, her voice barely audible. Her throat was parched, and she desperately wanted a drink. 'Hermione? Is that you?'

There was no reply save for the rustling of paper and scurrying of feet. Julie put her head down on the pillow and gave into sleep.

By evening, Hermione was preparing supper, but could not hide her concern that Maggie had not yet returned.

'I understood they were only having a short ride today,' she said. 'I expected them home long before supper.'

'Don't worry, Herm,' said her husband, attempting to allay her fears while concealing his own concern. 'She'll be safe with Smokey, we know that. They've probably called in at some of his mates or are chin-wagging with some of the drovers.' But he did not sound convincing.

As Hermione served supper, a worn-out Julie appeared.

'Hey, Julie, how are you feeling now?' enquired her host. 'Would you like some tucker?'

'I feel better now, thanks,' she replied a little weakly. 'Sorry to be such a nuisance. It was the smell of cooking that got me out of bed. I'm famished.'

She tucked into a plate of Hermione's special lamb hot pot, and was almost finished when she remarked, 'Isn't Maggie eating with us tonight?'

Jett and Hermione locked eyes and wondered about telling their still fragile guest the news of Maggie's absence.

After a brief pause, Jett said as calmly as he could, 'They haven't returned yet. We expected them long before now actually, and it's getting dark.'

Hermione continued, 'We're getting worried. It's not like Smokey to have a guest out for so long on a first ride.'

Julie stopped eating and took in the enormity of what was happening.

Seeing the concern on both women's faces, Jett stood up. 'Look, gals,' he said, 'I'll gather some of the guys and we'll ride out and have a dekko. There's bound to be a simple explanation for them being late. It's going to be dark soon.'

He left his meal unfinished, patted his wife's back in a reassuring gesture and smiled at Julie as he left the kitchen.

Shortly after, a posse of riders, under Jett's direction, took off to explore the vast area. 'I know Smokey's usual route for guest riders,' he directed them. 'We'll head for Wild Creek, and if there's no sign of them we'll split up and branch out. Does everyone have power torches, flares, and mobile phones? We know the signal can get lost the further out we go but keep in touch as best you can. They can't have gone far. Something must have gone wrong, so let's go get 'em.'

With no sign of the duo around Wild Creek, Jett split the stockmen into groups and gave directions as to where to ride. Darkness now made the journey treacherous, but the drovers were experienced and knew the area so well that they could ride almost anywhere under any conditions.

Each group reported in as instructed; no sighting had been made of the two riders. Jett was becoming more and more alarmed.

'If something has happened to Smokey, Maggie will be at a loss to find her way back,' he said. 'It's essential we keep searching.'

After what felt like an eternity, one of the drovers called to his mate, 'Shush, can you hear something coming towards us? Listen. Well, I'll be jiggered, if it ain't someone singing!'

They stilled their horses and listened. In the distance, and coming towards them, was the unmistakable rendering of *Waltzing Matilda*. A few minutes later, from the darkness, the lost riders appeared. Smokey was on foot leading Dandy Boy, with the unruffled Maggie astride the horse, both singing their heads off. 'Woah,' called Smokey as Dandy Boy came to a halt. 'It sure is fair dinkum to see you blokes. We hoped someone would come for us. Windsor lost a shoe way back there, so we had to lead him slowly back to the drover's station. He needed to rest up. They'll see to him in the morning and bring him home. We've had a long trek back. Dandy Boy wouldn't hear tell of me riding with Maggie… one or other, he seemed to be telling me! So, it was a long, slow journey. We lost the phone signal back there.'

One of the stockmen addressed Maggie, 'Are you alright, ma'am?'

'Never better,' she replied. 'I've had the best adventure of my life.'

Word soon reached the other searchers that all was well, and they returned to the station to be greeted warmly by Hermione and Julie.

'What an adventure we've had,' said an exhausted Maggie. 'I'm dying for a cup of tea. Julie, how are you now? You look much better than you did during the night.'

'Much relieved to see you back safely,' said her friend. 'I'm fine, thanks.'

∞

Life continued in a whirlwind of activities for the visitors, and they looked forward to the Saturday get-together and entertainment and meeting up with the many ranch hands and visitors. Jett introduced them to a young couple who had recently arrived from Spain for a farm-stay visit.

'Come on, you gals, and meet some other home-stay folk,' laughed their host. 'You folks need to stick together among us Aussies.'

The young couple, Max and Val García, declared themselves to be students on a gap year. Rather shyly, Val shook hands and spoke almost in a whisper.

Julie, always astute, noticed that the girl's hands were sweaty and hot. She seemed uncomfortable and appeared not to want to linger in their company, leaving the talking to her partner who was confident and carried himself well. He looked to be in his early 30s, and Julie thought he looked rather old to be a student but gave it no more thought.

'I'm Max,' he said, shaking hands with Maggie and then Julie. 'Good to meet you.' He spoke in perfect English, with a slight European accent.

He was more forthcoming than Val and gave an air of confidence as he explained how they hoped to spend their gap year.

'We plan to spend a month or two here, then head off to do some backpacking. We'd like to make our way across to Perth. I hear it's a beautiful city. We've been here for a few days, but Val didn't feel like joining in the Saturday entertainment. The flight was too long for her; she hates flying at the best of times and hasn't really recovered from it. And she isn't comfortable among strangers. We had a go at herding cattle, but again, she was petrified when the cattle came too close for comfort.'

Julie wondered why the timid girl had come to be in the ranch in the first place. She could read people very well and felt something was not quite right with this couple. Her inquisitive mind went into overdrive as she determined to probe a bit more.

'Don't you think there is something strange about that kid, Val?' she asked Maggie, as they sat together drinking wine in the ranch house kitchen.

'Can't say I noticed anything, but then you, with your runaway imagination, will no doubt spot something that the rest of us haven't observed.' Maggie smiled. 'I think she's probably just a shy person.'

'Mm,' muttered Julie, obviously not convinced with her friend's theory. 'We need to keep our eyes open. She's hiding something, and I'm going to get to the bottom of it. She avoids eye contact; it's more than shyness. At the next barbeque, you try and involve her in conversation and report anything unusual.'

Maggie laughed at her friend's enthusiasm for investigating something that others wouldn't notice, 'Over and out, detective. Will do.'

An unexpected opportunity arose for Maggie to speak to the quiet student, when the young girl called at the main house to ask for a train timetable from Bathurst. Maggie was alone in the kitchen, having volunteered to do some baking to allow Hermione time to deal with other household chores, when Val tentatively knocked on the door.

'Hello. Val, isn't it? Come into the kitchen. I'm keeping my eye on the baking. Would you like a cup of tea, I've just put the kettle on?'

The girl hesitated, unsure how to respond to Maggie's welcoming smile. But the smell of newly-baked bread and Maggie's friendly approach put her at ease, and she found herself hugging a mug of tea and sampling some home baking.

Maggie, aware of the girl's shyness, chatted on about everything and anything, and watched as the girl relaxed slightly.

'I'll fetch a timetable for you,' she said. 'Jett keeps them over here. Are you taking a train ride then?'

Val hesitated, mumbled something incoherently, then burst into tears. Immediately, Maggie went to her and put a motherly arm around the shaking girl.

'Oh, what on earth is troubling you, my dear? You're shaking all over. Are you in pain?'

'No, no,' wept the girl, as she accepted a tissue. 'It's... it's... Oh, I want to go home. I should never have agreed to come here.'

As she put her head on Maggie's shoulder and gave vent to her distress, the older woman comforted her by making gentle shushing sounds as she had done so often with her own children. Once the girl's sobs had subsided enough for her to breathe normally, Val apologised for the trouble she had caused, stood up, and headed for the door.

'Sorry, sorry, I have to go,' she said. 'He'll be angry with me. He'll punish me.' And she sprinted off before Maggie could say or do anything.

Poor kid, she thought. *Julie is right, there is something going on here.*

Reluctant to discuss it with anyone other than Julie, Maggie waited until they were alone before relating the incident.

'She's obviously very unhappy and scared of something. She made a remark about Max being angry with her. At least, I presume she was referring to Max,' whispered Maggie, knowing that the kitchen area was usually a hive of activity, where people came and went at will. She didn't want anyone overhearing their conversation. 'Her accent changed remarkably from slightly European to most definitely English. I would say Mancunian.'

Julie looked thoughtful. 'We'll keep our eye on things,' she replied. 'I knew something was amiss.'

∞

With only over a week left of their holiday, the visitors took full advantage of the time to ride out with Smokey to visit

Jett's parents and Uncle Barney. Julie was surprised at her own capabilities and enjoyed riding along on Jasper, an affable horse, which was docile and at ease with his rider. Maggie once more rode Dandy Boy – the two had become firm friends.

As they rode, Smokey told them tales of his boyhood and early life with his family.

'My father was a farrier. We moved around from one ranch to another when work dried up, and I learned the trade from him. When my parents passed away, I continued to roam but soon felt the need to settle. I arrived here by chance when Jett was taking on more hands, and he gave me a job. I put down roots and love the life, wouldn't want to be anywhere else. Jett is great to work for, he's an ace guy, and the stockmen have the greatest respect for him. There's plenty of work to be done here, so I guess I'll spend the rest of my days in this part of the world.'

Julie said, 'I can feel how this place could draw you in, it's spectacular. I'll be sorry to leave, not just the area but the people. Everyone we've met has been so friendly and helpful.'

'That's one thing about the steading, we get to meet lots of people from every walk of life,' continued Smokey. 'The students on gap year generally throw themselves into the life here, and surely go home that bit more mature, in my view. The shy ones come out of their shell. I've seen kids who wouldn't say boo but they've morphed into stronger characters by the time they leave.'

'Talking of shy kids, have you noticed the young girl, Val, around the place, Smokey? Did she show any interest in horse riding, for example?' asked Maggie. 'She came to the house the other day while I was in the kitchen doing some baking and seemed to be uptight about something. She burst into tears and ran off. It was very strange indeed.'

Smokey shook his head. 'Can't say I've noticed her around much,' he said. 'She didn't mix with the others and stayed close to her boyfriend. He seemed an ace guy, worked hard with the others helping mend the fences at the top field, said Val had a headache and was resting. I had the feeling the kid was out of her depth here.'

Maggie turned to Julie and smiled. 'I smell a case for investigation here, my inquisitive author friend.'

Julie laughed. 'I'm sure there's something sinister going on. It may be, as you say, she's probably just a shy kid who is homesick. I'll have a word with her at the next barbeque and report back... over and out!' She looked thoughtful. 'She seems much younger than Max, doesn't she?'

When they reached the cabin where Barney lived, he sat on the veranda rocking back and forth on his wicker chair, puffing on his well-used pipe, and stroking an elderly dog that lay contentedly at his feet.

'How do, ladies?' he called as he rose to greet them, the fang tooth wobbling as he spoke. 'Join me in a sip of grog.'

They group spent some time there listening to Barney's tales, including how he had tamed a stock horse that no-one else seemed able to handle.

'I have the gift, you see, I'm the best horse-whisperer this side of the valley,' he confided. 'Sure, folks used to bring their steeds for me to tame. I remember once—'

'Sorry, Barney,' Smokey interrupted. 'You'll have to keep your tale until the barbie. I've got to get the ladies back to the ranch. We don't want folks worrying if we turn up late, like last time.'

The women said their goodbyes with a promise of catching up with him next day at what would be their last barbeque, then the trio rode back together and stabled the horses. Julie and Maggie, after a welcome drink, freshened up and joined the others for supper.

'Hey, tomorrow is going to be your last barbie with us,' said Jett, as he poured some wine for the ladies. 'We'll be sorry to see you go, it's been fair dinkum having you with us. Hermione sure loved having you gals here, wish you could stay on. We'll make the barbie extra special and send you off with a bang,' he laughed, as if hiding a secret from them.

∞

Next day, the visitors spent the time helping Hermione prepare for the evening barbeque and chatted as if they would never talk again.

As they worked together, Hermione said, 'Jett's parents are coming over early to say their goodbyes before the rabble arrive for the barbie. I want to show them my treasures, too. They've heard me talk about them, and Lilybud especially is keen to see what Jonny has sent over.'

No sooner had she spoken than the elderly couple arrived accompanied by Brad, who had fetched them over in the Land Rover.

'G'avro, ladies,' said Stan. 'Lovely afternoon. Sure sorry to see you gals go, been fair dinkum to have you here.'

'We've had a fabulous time, thanks, Stan,' said Maggie. 'It's been good to meet you both, and it will be hard to tear ourselves away from Oz.'

They chatted for some time before Hermione said she would fetch the box from the safe to let them see her treasures. 'Lilybud, you will love them,' she said.

She returned with the box and placed it carefully on the table. She unwrapped the hessian cloth that covered it, opened the box, and stood looking at what was in front of her, her face drained of colour as she shook her head in total amazement. 'Jett!' she called out. 'Jett, come here!'

Jett, his arm around his distraught wife, looked in anger at the almost empty box. Some items had been removed and replaced with stones to fool them into thinking the box was intact.

'I'm stonkered, absolutely bemused. How can this be? Brad,' he called to his son, 'do you still have your key? Herm, honey, yours is in the box. I have mine right here, and there are no others.'

Brad produced his key to the safe and placed it beside the other two.

'What's happened?' he asked, shaking his head as he hugged his weeping mother. 'My key is always safely pinned in my pocket, never out of sight.'

The group gathered around the almost empty container. Maggie's face strained at the loss of the treasures that she had so anxiously carried across the miles.

'Who could have done this?' exclaimed Julie, her mind whizzing with questions. She examined the box. 'There are still some pieces left,' she said, 'as if whoever did this was disturbed and had to leave in a hurry.'

'But who had access to our keys?' questioned Brad. 'Only we three know the safe combination, so... who?'

'Close the kitchen door, Herm, we want to keep this private among ourselves,' said a subdued Jett. 'Everyone, sit around the table here and catch your breath and let's puzzle this out.' He swiftly took control. 'Brad, fetch your mother a drink. In fact, get one for all of us. We sure need it. The things have gone walkabout. Someone wants to make a pile of moolah selling them on.' Jett's parents were as distressed as the others at what seemed to be a serious crime.

'In all the years I've been here,' began Stan, 'we've never had any crime, apart from some petty pilfering that the stockmen soon put a stop to. But nothing, nothing like this, ever.'

They sat in silence, each one thinking of the horror inflicted on them by a callous thief.

Eventually, Jett spoke. 'Can you think, any of you, of anything to help here? Any suspicions about anyone on the homestead, among the ranchers, the vacation students? Anything, however small, to shed light on this damned business?'

Maggie, wiping tears from her eyes, ventured, 'We,' she nodded towards Julie, 'wondered about the young couple, Max and Val. There is something not quite right with the girl; she's afraid of something or someone.'

She related the incident when the girl had fled in terror from the kitchen. 'She kept repeating, *He will be angry with me. He'll punish me.* She seemed to be afraid of someone, Max I presume, yet he seems protective of her,' she explained. 'I can't see him being vicious, but I've not had an opportunity to speak to her since.'

Julie added, 'We were going to make a point of talking to her at the barbie.'

Jett turned to his wife and son and asked hesitantly, 'Have either of you inadvertently mentioned the jewels to anyone? Please think. Someone knew about the safe and its combination.'

Brad said, 'Milly knew about the jewels, as you know, but she has no knowledge of the safe combination.'

Jett clapped his son's shoulder. 'We know that, son, but she's one of the most honest people we've ever met, so you can stop worrying. Milly isn't a suspect.'

'Oh!' exclaimed Julie, as if a light had suddenly been switched on in her head. 'This might be relevant. Do you remember the day I had a migraine? The day Maggie went riding and arrived home late? I woke up with a dreadful thirst and heard someone moving about the kitchen. I called out for water, thinking, Hermione, that you were there, but no-one answered and then I was aware of rustling paper and someone scurrying off. I fell asleep again and have only remembered the incident just now. Do you think it could have happened then?'

Jett shrugged. 'Quite likely. No-one would expect anyone to be in the house at that time of day, and you know we have an open door to allow access to the kitchen for anyone who wants cold drinks from the fridge. It would be quite easy for someone to locate the safe, but who knew the combination? That's the puzzling thing. The combination is known to only three of us.'

A tearful Hermione said, 'I had reassured Julie that I'd be around the house that day, should she need me, as I was doing some paper work. I've only now remembered that I left for about twenty minutes after someone phoned to say some sheep had escaped from the west field. I drove there only to find that all was well, and I presumed the drovers had returned them to the field. I thought no more about it until now.'

'This could be quite significant, it fits in with what Julie heard coming from the kitchen. Someone set this up.' Brad thumped the table as he spoke, his anger clear for all to see. 'Dad, we need to get the police here, this is more serious than petty thieving. Mother, did you recognise the voice?'

'No, Brad,' she shook her head sadly. 'Remember how many people are on this ranch. I could not possibly distinguish one voice from another, and the call was short and abrupt.'

Hermione was an emotional wreck. It was as if the heist had awakened in her a loss, not only of the precious items, but of her last link with her mother and her former life at Chestermere Hall. Jett tried to comfort her by reminding her that not all the pieces had gone and that she still had the lovely miniatures in her room. But she was inconsolable, her grief evident to everyone.

'Who could be so despicable?' she kept saying. 'Who has done this to us?'

∞

Maggie put her arms around her sister-in-law as she cried. Holding back her own sobs, she tried to reassure Hermione that they would get to the bottom of the mess.

'If I know Julie Sinclair,' she said, 'she will stop at nothing to solve this and bring the perpetrators to justice. She has a nose for this kind of thing.'

Julie nodded in agreement. 'I have a gut feeling that Max and Val are involved somewhere,' she told them. 'My gut hasn't let me down yet, but it's a case of proving it. Don't worry, we will have this solved.'

'I'll call the police now,' Jett assured everyone, 'but you know how long it will take them to drive over. Meanwhile, Brad, during the barbie could you search the accommodation blocks? Look for anything unusual, be discreet, and don't disturb anything.'

'Can Maggie and I help with the search?' asked Julie, her heart going out to the tearful Hermione.

Jett shook his head. 'Best for you two gals to be seen around. After all, folks will want to say farewell. Maggie and Hermione, you must call Jonny and put him in the loop. He'll be devastated, but it's best that he knows what has happened. Take a moment to compose yourselves, though, you don't want him to hear how upset you are.'

The two went off to make their difficult call while Julie, ever practical, announced, 'We have a barbie to organise. I'll get on with final preparations, it will keep my mind off things.'

'I'll help you,' whispered an obviously distraught Lilybud, while Stan set about collecting plates and cutlery.

Jonny was understandably shocked and upset at the turn of events and attempted to console his wife and sister with assurances that the culprit would be found and dealt with.

'Herm, get me the contact for the chief detective once you have reported this theft. Explain who I am,' he said. 'It might carry a bit of weight to the investigation when they know they are dealing with a member of Her Majesty's Government. Maggie, darling, don't be upset. I am determined a second heist will not take as long to solve as the first one. You have Julie with you. She has a detective's nose for solving crime, so fear not, my dear. Trust her gut instincts on this. All will be well.'

While a referendum some years previously had shown a desire among a minority of Australians to break ties with the British monarchy, especially after a serious of royal scandals, the trend had reversed in recent years. With the emergence of young, vibrant royals, more citizens had shown a desire to retain the monarchy. For this reason, Jonny hoped the mention of his status might bring a serious element to the solving of the crime. He remained calm during the distressing phone call and reassured his wife that she should not harbour any guilt.

'You did everything by the book, darling, you kept the box by your side and delivered it safely. You know everything was intact when Hermione opened it in front of you all. So, you have nothing to blame yourself for, my dear.'

That evening, the barbeque went ahead, despite the dreadful crime. As it was to be the last before the visitors left for home, Jett gave an amusing talk in which he thanked Julie and Maggie for their company over the past weeks and for the help they had given around the homestead.

'We will gloss over the incident when Maggie and Smokey were late coming back from a ride,' he joked. 'We will spare you Maggie's rendition of *Waltzing Matilda!*'

The crowd roared with laughter as Jett continued regaling them with fun incidents from their stay.

Julie and Maggie spent the evening going among the folks, saying goodbye and sharing stories, and listening once more to Barney's tales of bravado. At the same time, Brad quietly searched as many apartments and bunkhouses as he could. He found nothing to arouse concern.

He moved to another accommodation block and found the door to one of them ajar. He knocked and, receiving no reply, entered quietly to find the room empty of all personal items, clothes and luggage. The bed had not been slept in and the room was left tidy as if the occupants had prepared it ready for the next set of visitors.

Brad sought out Julie, called her aside and whispered, 'The couple you mentioned appear to have gone. Their room is empty of everything.'

Julie went with him to see for herself the apartment used by Max and Val. She had a look around. It was as if no-one had ever been there.

'Well, they have most certainly gone for good,' she said. 'That adds to my suspicion about those two.'

As she turned to leave the room, she noticed on the floor by the bed a small comb, which had obviously been missed when they were packing.

'This might come in handy,' she said as she wrapped it in a clean tissue. 'Brad, let your father know of this development.'

Jett was puzzled as to how the kids, as he saw them, had managed to leave the homestead unobserved.

'There was no-one scheduled to drive off-ranch today, so how did they leave?' he mused. 'They can't have walked off. Brad, check the vehicles, see if any of them have been moved.'

Julie returned to the party to quietly inform Maggie and Hermione of their findings. A few minutes later Brad, breathless and obviously incensed, joined them to report that one of the vehicles, a small pickup, was missing.

'Where are the keys kept?' asked Julie.

'In the vehicle,' replied Brad. 'We leave them in the trucks, as it saves time hunting for them. We've never had problems with it. Until now.'

The barbeque, true to form, lasted well into the wee small hours, but eventually the revellers returned to their various accommodation. The family, distressed beyond words, gathered around the kitchen table, too tired to sleep and determined to explore all possibilities of the theft.

Julie started. 'I think the finger of guilt must point to Max and Val who appear to have run off using a pickup truck. I'm sure of it. What other explanation could there be?'

Discussion and theories led nowhere, and only posed yet more questions. Eventually, the group retired for the night to catch a few hours' sleep before another busy day crept up on them.

At breakfast, Jett took a call from the State police asking that no-one leave the compound until officers arrived, possibly the next day – or more likely the day after that. Jett explained that his sister-in-law and her friend were booked to fly back to UK, and that any delay would disrupt their ongoing connecting flight and would not be acceptable.

He added, 'We're talking about the wife of a high-profile member of the UK government. It is imperative that these women fly to Britain as arranged. They have commitments to honour.' After much to-ing and fro-ing and calls to superior officers, it was agreed that Julie and Maggie should leave the homestead a day earlier than planned to meet with officers for interview.

That day was a round of frantic packing, hasty goodbyes, and special wishes to Milly for a safe delivery for the impending birth. The women had been assured that they would not miss their flight and that overnight accommodation would be provided for them.

'As long as it's not in a prison cell,' laughed Julie, attempting to lighten the concern for everyone.

Maggie was particularly upset. Having delivered the box safely and relieved to be free of the responsibility, she now struggled to shake off a feeling of guilt.

Jett and Hermione travelled with them to meet with police officers, leaving the ranch in the capable hands of their son. The journey back to Bathurst was more subdued than that of their arrival, and the only comments came from Jett as he attempted to lighten the mood as they passed interesting landmarks.

As they drove into the airport parking area where they were to meet with police officers, Hermione suddenly called out, 'Jett, look over there! That's our pickup truck, over there by the wall.'

There, among other parked vehicles, was the unmistakable truck, identified by the various bumps and scratches acquired over years of driving on rough terrain. Jett jumped out, checked it over, and retrieved the keys which were still in the vehicle.

Julie called to him, 'There will be prints on the keys, Jett. Best wrap them up until they can be checked out, and the vehicle will need dusted for prints.'

'There speaks an expert sleuth,' commented Maggie, who was proud of her friend's past crime-solving skills.

After alerting the officers to the pickup truck, which was then cordoned off with crime scene tape, the group explained their suspicions about the young students. They were shown to a waiting area and introduced to two officers who took statements from each of them in private.

'We were under the impression that the couple were students who were backpacking across Australia, planning to finish in Perth where they were to fly to Spain, where they said they lived and studied,' said Hermione during her interview.

She related all she knew of them, but details were scanty. 'Their application to join us appeared in order and didn't flag up any problems. We encourage students to spend time on the ranch to enrich their life experience. We've never had trouble before. I admit, we took them at face value.'

Jett related how the couple had not been particularly forthcoming when pressed about their life.

'I try to get to know the vacation students and make them welcome,' he explained. 'The boy – man, really – appeared to be the spokesperson for them both. He looked much older than he claimed to be, but I never questioned it; it didn't ring any bells. Val spoke little and seemed anxious. I didn't push for her to speak. Some kids are in awe of the vastness of the homestead and can suffer from travel weariness. When we realised the truck was missing, I never thought we would see it again. I presumed that it was being driven to wherever the kids planned to travel to.'

'The truck will be removed for prints and I'll have someone drive it back to your ranch when we're done,' said one of the officers. 'I'll arrange for an officer to take prints from all of you for elimination purposes. The key may have prints that can be lifted, too. From what you say, there's a real mystery as to how they got hold of your safe combination, that is, if they are our suspects. We could be chasing a red herring.'

'That's a possibility,' agreed Jett, 'but it's very suspicious, don't you think, that they took off shortly after the theft? If they had been unhappy and wanted to leave, we sure wouldn't have held them back and someone would have driven them into town.'

Maggie related the encounter with Val when the girl had run off in tears from the kitchen. 'She was distressed, but more than that, she was fearful of something, or someone. I thought, too, that her accent was false,' she told the officers. 'When she was upset, she resorted to what seemed to me to be a Manchester or northern UK accent. It was as if she had dropped her guard and wasn't aware of it.' 'Thank you all for your co-operation,' said the senior officer. 'I know where to find you if I require further assistance. Ladies, I believe your flight doesn't leave for twenty-four hours. If we have anything to report before then, we will be in touch.'

Julie finished her statement and joined the others in time to check in for their overnight stay. Jett and Hermione decided to book into the hotel and have a last meal and brainstorming session with them.

'This has been a sad ending to your holiday,' said Jett, 'but be assured that we will bring the thieves to task. I for one won't let this go until we have solved the matter.'

At breakfast the next morning, the hotel manager alerted Jett to a request from the police officer for them to join him in the security wing of the airport.

'He says he has something of interest to show you.'

On arrival, they gathered in a small room where CCTV cameras showed the airport compound. 'This is the control hub where these guys and gals monitor the entire airport,' explained the officer as he pointed to the people working at the screens. 'After you left last evening, I had them check CCTV from the past few days, and found what might, just might, be your couple. Chester, bring up what you found.'

With a flick of his fingers across the keyboard, Chester, a young dark-haired guy with a neatly trimmed beard, nodded and highlighted a group of passengers who were crossing the concourse.

'Check this out, do you recognise your two students?' asked the officer, as he moved to let Jett and the others have a better view of the grainy monitor. Chester moved the mouse slowly along a crowd of people milling around the concourse.

'Stop, there, just there!' called Julie. 'Can you go back a bit, please? Look, is that them? Jett, what do you think?'

'It *is* our two students,' he agreed. 'The bloke is recognisable, but can you bring up the picture? I want to see the girl's features a bit clearer.'

'I'll try,' said Chester, 'but we might lose definition. Bear with me.'

The others stared intently at the monitor as Chester carefully filled the frame with the picture.

'Yes!' cried Maggie. 'That's them.'

'Without a doubt,' replied Julie, 'that's Val and Max. She always seemed to walk with her head down and her shoulders hunched.'

Hermione nodded in agreement.

The officer thanked them for their assistance and contacted airport authorities to verify the details of the two travellers picked out by the group. He later reported that none of the passenger lists showed the names Max and Val García.

'Oh,' said an incredulous Julie. 'Those pictures were so like the couple. I'd bet my last dollar on it. Something is wrong here, very wrong.'

'Don't worry, ma'am,' reassured the officer. 'The authorities at Sydney have been alerted and are checking passenger arrival CCTV and are searching for those people. We may be too late to locate them. They could be anywhere by now.'

'Are we chasing the wrong people?' asked a confused Hermione. 'We could be wasting everyone's time. The pictures on the monitor aren't really clear enough for us to be sure it is Max and Val, are they?'

'Don't get despondent, Herm, we need to find these kids, and soon,' Jett told her. 'If they are the people who stole your jewels, we must find them, and quickly. Don't forget that you still have several of the items, as well as the little miniatures in your room. It sounds as if Julie disturbed them by calling out from her sickbed, so you haven't lost everything. Don't you want them brought to justice?'

'Of course, I do. But I would feel bad if we were accusing innocent people.'

Jett was determined to have the couple on the monitor apprehended, if only to eliminate them from enquiries. The senior police officer informed him that he would contact him as soon as there was any development on the case of the missing jewels and other precious artefacts.

'The photographs you took of the items will help the investigation, thank you for thinking smart,' he said.

As time drew closer to Maggie and Julie's flight to Sydney, the group said their farewells with emotions running high. Maggie, still distressed at the turn of events, felt guilty that she had let Jonny down. But they reassured her that even if Jonny had made the trip, the heist would probably still have happened.

During their hour-long flight, Maggie was silent and thoughtful. Julie left her to her thoughts while she herself went over everything in her mind. In Sydney, they spent a quiet night at a hotel to rest and prepare for the long flight home.

In the early hours of the morning, Maggie, who had tossed and turned for several hours, awoke and lay sobbing quietly. Julie, also awake, came from her room to join her.

'Oh Julie, I've made a mess of what was to be a holiday of a lifetime for you. I'm so miserable and saddened at letting everyone down.'

Julie could see that her friend was spiralling into depression. Maggie was normally a calm, unruffled person, one who shrugged off any difficulties that came her way, but she looked and seemed vulnerable.

'Maggie dear, please, please, you must rid those thoughts from your mind. You did what was asked of you. You could not have done more,' Julie insisted. 'The way you guarded that box was formidable; no-one could have prised it from you. Hermione got her treasured box delivered safely, and Jonny was relieved that it had been so. No-one could have foreseen that some of the contents would be stolen. Sure, everyone is upset, and we'll leave no stone unturned to find the culprits and see that justice is meted out.'

'Julie, we can't do a thing about this,' sobbed Maggie. 'How can we? We must rely on the Aussie police, as they have the resources. We are helpless. And what can we do from the other side of the world?'

'You're right,' Julie nodded, 'we can't do anything, but we know someone in high places who might put out a few feelers.'

'Are you thinking of Jonny, by any chance?'

'Yes. I am. With his connections, he could help in some way.'

'He has already asked to be kept in touch with the Aussie police.'

They talked well into the night, by which time, Maggie, more composed, settled to sleep. Julie, her mind in overdrive, sipped a drink from the mini-bar as she mused over events that had turned the holiday into a nightmare.

The long flight home was uneventful, the excitement of the return journey paling into insignificance compared to their outward flight. They arrived reasonably refreshed and were met at the airport by Jonny, who hugged them both and quickly loaded the luggage into his car, explaining that he had only a few more minutes left of parking time.

'We'll head over to the hotel and you can tell me everything,' he said.

∞

Over a light meal, the women took it in turns to relay the events leading to the theft of the jewellery. Jonny listened attentively as he held his wife's hand to reassure her that all would be well.

'I had a long telephone conversation with the senior officer in charge, who filled me in on the latest development,' he told them. 'It seems that your two young people vanished after arriving at Bathurst Airport. The police are checking CCTV in the city and have an alert out for them. They are also searching back records of arrivals at Sydney Airport. Maggie darling, you must not dwell on it. Leave it to the Sydney police. Now, girls,' he smiled to lighten the mood a little, 'tell me about my wayward sister and her homestead. I believe young Bradley has found himself a wife and is soon to be a father. How the years go by!'

∞

Back home, Julie drove to her friend Liz's pound to collect her beloved dog. The memory of a previous time when she'd called to collect her three dogs and become embroiled in their tragic loss, played on her mind. She drove slowly into the compound, past the colourful *Safe Haven* sign, and on into the main yard. A cacophony of barks met her as she parked her vehicle.

Liz, looking dishevelled as usual, greeted her warmly, as did her pet. But once satisfied that she had acknowledged him, he returned to play in the paddock that Liz and her husband Colin had set out as a canine exercise assault course.

'Come on then, girl,' Liz urged, 'tell me all about your Oz adventure. Was it wonderful?'

Over coffee in the garden, Julie described the homestead, the barbeque evenings, and their riding experience with Smokey, then related the sad tale of the theft of the precious articles. Liz sat with her mouth open in disbelief, aghast as the story unfolded, and shook her head in disgust.

'Oh, how dreadful, and after the care you both took to deliver the box safely. I can only imagine the pain that caused. Poor Maggie, she must be bereft, and Hermione, too. How awful. Have there been any developments in the investigation?'

Julie shook her head. 'Jonny is in regular communication with the senior officer in charge of the case and speaks to his sister several times a week. They are both devastated at the loss of family heirlooms for a second time.'

'History repeating itself,' sighed Liz, as she tried to make sense of what Julie had related. 'Once more, unto the breach, dear Julie...' Liz shook her long, tangled hair as she spoke, pulling out bits of dog hair. 'You must put your investigative skills to the test and solve the heist for the second time. You have a nose for such things.'

Julie, watching Liz, put her coffee cup down quickly and stood up. 'Liz, you darling, thank you, thank you.' She called for her pooch to ride back with her. Briefly taking in the surprised look on her friend's face, she explained quickly, 'You and your unruly hair! Thank you! I've suddenly remembered the comb. Must rush.'

Leaving a bewildered Liz standing at the gate, Julie drove off as if she were on a mission, as indeed she was. Hardly taking time to pick up the mail that had accumulated during her absence, she stepped over the pile of letters on the mat and rummaged through her unpacked luggage until she found the comb that she had retrieved from the homestead.

I had totally forgotten about this. Well done, Liz, and your tangled mess. It reminded me that I hadn't handed the comb to the officers.

She wasted no time in contacting Maggie to tell of her discovery. Jonny, she knew, was involved in an overseas conference as part of his ministerial post and would be unable to take her call.

'If we can have it tested for DNA, it might throw some light on our culprits,' she suggested.

Maggie, delighted to have even a miniscule of hope, was happier than she had been since her return home. Her guilt, while quite unfounded, was still raw and Julie's enthusiasm had raised her spirits. She found herself humming as she continued with some tasks in hand. *I am impatient to hear from Jonny. He will be delighted with Julie's find.*

Julie, now more composed, settled her dog, Curley, to his food then cycled back to Liz's place to apologise. 'Liz, you must think me such a mad woman to rush off without an explanation,' she said.

'Julie, I've known you long enough to understand that when you have a bee in your bonnet, it's better to let you get on with whatever gets you so fired up. Wine? Talk?'

Over a glass of wine in Liz's cosy, if messy, sitting room, Julie explained about the find of the comb and its possible implications for the investigation.

'Things haven't progressed much since we left Oz, but this might just kick-start it. It's truly amazing what information can be discovered from such a tiny piece of material.'

They talked well into the evening, and just as Julie made a move to go home, Colin arrived to greet her with a welcome home hug.

'Do you have to go now?' he asked. 'I want to hear about your Aussie adventure.'

'Well, I guess I could stay and fill you in on my trip. Curley is settled for the night, there won't be a peep out of him until morning,'

'That's perfect,' said Liz. 'I'll rustle up some supper while you and Colin have a chat. The spare room is ready for you to kip in.'

Julie smiled inwardly, aware that Liz's idea of a room being ready was quite different from her own.

The three chatted into the small hours, discussing the heist of the jewels and brainstorming how it could have come about. Julie told of her suspicions about the couple, Max and Val, and the search for them in Bathurst and Sydney.

Eventually, sleep called. Colin took the few rescue dogs for a last quick sprint before settling them, then himself, for a night's sleep.

A few days later, Julie woke to the incessant ringing of her phone.

'Julie,' said an excited Jonny, 'I hope I haven't wakened you. I know it's rather early, but I have to be off again soon.'

'No problem, Jonny, I've overslept yet again. Since returning from Oz, my body clock is at sixes and sevens.'

'Maggie is the same,' he laughed. 'She's turning night into day. Now, my dear, firstly, let me thank you for the find of the comb. I'm hopeful it will lead us further on in the investigation. Maggie is coming to London soon to meet me; we seldom see each other now that I've been promoted. We both wondered if you would care to join us, if you are free to do so. It would be an opportunity to hand over the comb for DNA testing. I had a word with an expert who will see to it, and Maggie will enjoy your company if I'm called away.'

'Jonny, I would be delighted,' said Julie, now fully awake. 'I was wondering how to get the comb safely to you.'

Once more, Julie's pet was deposited with Liz.

'I love having dogs around me as you know, and yours loves it here at his holiday home,' laughed Liz. She renewed acquaintance with Curley, who fussed over her as if he had been away for a lengthy period.

'You know, Liz, my dog will think that you are his owner and I'm a part-time carer. I really have to get him a playmate.'

'Look no further than Topsy, our golden Labrador-of-sorts, they seem to have taken a shine to each other. I'd be glad for you to have him, knowing he's going to a good home, even if it is only part-time,' chuckled Liz.

On hearing his name, Topsy, sporting a rather lopsided grin, bounced up to Julie as if accepting her as his new owner, and demanding to be fussed over by her.

'That's settled then,' Julie laughed. 'Curley and Topsy! Sounds a good combination.'

Before Julie left for London, she called in at her local post office to send off a few letters, and was warmly welcomed by Jessica Morris, the local postmistress, who welcomed her with a barrage of questions.

'It's good to see you home, my dear. Did you have a good holiday? How was the weather? Was it too hot for you? My sister couldn't stand the heat over there. Will you write a book about your travels?'

Jessica hardly paused for breath, nor did she give Julie time to reply. She felt it was her duty to the community to be the first to hear and pass on fresh news, and Julie's return from the other side of the world was, for her, an opening to do so.

'Jessica, lovely to see you, too. It was an interesting experience. Australia is beautiful, and I met some nice people. Can't linger, Jessica, I'm off to London soon to meet my friend, Maggie. I wanted to get these letters off as soon as possible.'

Julie had no intention of mentioning the theft to her, as she knew the story would have escalated and grown arms and legs before she reached home.

'Maggie?' questioned Jessica. 'Wasn't she the friend you went to Australia with? Are you going to meet her so soon after returning home?'

Questions ricocheted from the lips of the incorrigible woman as she attempted to waylay her customer and drain every modicum of information.

'That's correct,' replied Julie, as she headed for the door.

'We have some unfinished business to see to.'

'Business?' questioned the postmistress, 'but I thought it was a leisure trip, not a business one.'

Julie smiled to herself as she bade farewell to the woman who, if allowed to do so, would extract every ounce of scandal and tittle-tattle.

'Bye, Jessica. I'll fill you in when I return, and show you some stunning pictures,' she said, and hurried off chuckling at the busybody's attempt to dig deeper.

∞

Jonny had wasted no time in contacting a forensic scientist – a man known to him, and whom he trusted to carry out DNA testing on the comb. Jack Adamson had explained about testing DNA samples and how the result could help solve crimes.

'There have been many examples over the years,' he told Jonny, 'of criminals being brought to justice – some after many, many years – as technology in the field of DNA understanding is progressing at a fast pace. Criminals who thought they had got away with, in some cases, murder, should be fearful of a knock on the door because science can catch up with them.' Jonny related the events surrounding the comb and asked what data could be obtained from it. 'It's a small comb and covered in hair. How can it be of help in the investigation?'

'It's amazing the detail we can extract from the hair, or from a few drops of blood, enough to get a good sample,' Jack said. 'If your suspects are on police records – even if they haven't been charged with an offence, and only arrested – there could be enough evidence on police national computer data to link DNA samples. I won't bore you with the scientific blurb, just to say STR – that's Short Tandem Repeat analysis, to do with how the analysis is broken up – can be matched to blood samples of a suspect. I've already contacted an Australian forensic scientist, Lyndon Craig, who is overseeing testing for this case.'

Jonny was fascinated to hear how scientific progress could nail a suspect and bring him or her to justice.

'You work in a very interesting field, Jack. It must have its rewards.'

Jack shrugged. 'Anything that helps get scum off the streets is fine by me. It's up to you chaps in your ivory tower in London to make the laws to keep them locked up,' he laughed.

∞

The apartment which Jonny used during his time in parliament was an exclusive riverside development on the banks of the mighty River Thames, within walking distance of the Palace of Westminster. He relished the opportunity to walk there and back, especially after a tiring day, and blow away the cobwebs of political concerns. It was his home during the time Parliament was in session, and Maggie often joined him there when time permitted.

Julie was thrilled to accept the invitation to visit them for a few days. The apartment was stunning: it consisted of three spacious ensuite bedrooms, a large lounge with views over the river, an office area near a compact kitchen, and a sheltered balcony where people could sit and watch the busy river come to life. It was obvious to Julie that Maggie had had a hand in the décor, from the drapes and wall mountings to the lamps that gave the apartment an exquisite finish.

With the comb duly handed over and sent off to Jack Adamson, Julie and Maggie were enjoying a chat with Jonny about his work as a member of Her Majesty's Government and were so engrossed in his travel tales that they failed to hear the apartment door open. Jonny, with his back to the river, sat facing the doorway.

'Jonny, 'said Maggie curiously, 'what are you grinning at? What has caught your attention?'

'Me!' called a voice from the doorway.

Maggie turned around and yelled, 'Robin! Robin! As she jumped up to greet her son, another voice announced, 'And me!'

'Letitia!' cried out the ecstatic mother. As she hugged and cried over her children, Jonny whispered to Julie, 'I set this up!'

Robin explained, 'We wanted to surprise you, so we spent the last two nights in a hotel to help us get over jet-lag and to catch up with each other.'

'And we prayed that we wouldn't bump into you in the interim,' added Letitia.

'You certainly surprised me. I'm pinching myself to see my beautiful children together under one roof.' Maggie was beaming with delight. 'Jonny, you scoundrel!' She accused her husband, 'You planned this, didn't you?'

Laughing heartily, Jonny nodded. 'I wanted us to be together, and for Julie to re-acquaint herself with our family.'

Robin hugged Julie, 'It's been a few years since we last saw you, Aunt Julie. Leticia and I wanted to personally thank you for the help you've given the family over the years.'

'Oh, Robin, please drop the *aunt,* just call me Julie. Yes, the last time we met, you were preparing for exams and told me of your interest in I.T. How you've grown!'

Robin was a delightful young man, with his mother's facial features and his father's height. He had an infectious grin, much like his father's. And, like the older man, oozed confidence.

Letitia, unfurled from her mother's hugs, wrapped herself around Julie.

'I remember you, Aunt Julie, sorry... Julie, although I was much younger than Robin when you came to our house. You helped me with a board game and you let me win.'

'Hah, did I now?' Julie scoffed. 'We must have a re-run of that! How lovely to see you, and to hear of your interesting work.'

Letitia took her height from her mother and reminded Julie of Maggie when she first knew her at school. The girl portrayed a calmness and confidence that endeared her to those who met her.

While they hugged and fussed over each other, Jonny produced a bottle of champagne.

'Let's celebrate this day, we don't see you two often enough,' he said, as he grinned proudly at his children. 'And who better to share it with than our esteemed writer, confidante, and dearest friend.'

Jonny had organised an outside caterer to provide dinner for the family.

'It's manic around this area on a Friday evening to book a dinner reservation,' he explained. 'This way, we can relax and catch up, without the noise and bustle of a restaurant.'

The family ate, drank, laughed, and shared stories. Before long, the talk came around to the theft of the jewellery.

'What's the latest on the heist?' asked Robin, as he tucked into his dessert of profiteroles.

'Jack Adamson, the forensic scientist I told you about, keeps in touch with his counterpart in Australia – an esteemed scientist by the name of Lyndon Craig,' his father explained. 'The officers have completed the dust-down of the truck that the alleged thieves took off in and have lifted prints from the hessian cover and the container that held the jewellery. The pieces of newspaper, too, were able to provide enough for analysis, and Jack is analysing a comb that Julie rescued. They are hopeful that the cells from all of these will generate enough to isolate information to link the couple to the crime. We now have to wait for the results.'

'Have they located the culprits?' asked Letitia of her father.

'Not yet, darling. They appear to have mingled with the crowds at the airport and have not been seen since. Our hope lies in results from the scientists and the police investigation. Those kids could be anywhere by now.'

Julie remained with the family for several days, enjoying laughter-filled outings to the shops, theatre, and museums. Jonny returned to his work, with a promise of spending time at Chestermere Hall before his children were due to return to their respective places of work.

Any feelings of guilt harboured by Maggie over the missing jewels had slowly dissipated in the company of Robin and Letitia – the perfect surprise plotted by her concerned husband. He'd contacted their son and told him, *your mother needs cheering up and you two would be the tonic she needs to lift the black cloud from her shoulders.*

'Leave it with me, Pop, I'll contact my baby sister and come up with a rescue plan. It's about time we got together anyway. Skype is okay for keeping in touch but doesn't compare to being there in person.'

Robin and his sister had duly arrived in London to surprise their mother. And renewing friendship with Julie, whom they held in high esteem, had been a bonus.

After their busy few days in London, Maggie returned to the family's country estate with her son and daughter, while Julie, totally refreshed, went back home to Yetts Bank to make a start on her next thriller.

∞

Chewing on the end of her pen as she made notes for her next book, Julie looked out of the window and absently watched her two dogs frolicking on the grass. She found it difficult to concentrate; her mind was still on the Australian heist as she mulled over the details of past events. *Where did those two vanish to? How could they evade the airport authorities and get on a plane without being spotted on camera? Why were they not detected at the airport?* She returned to her writing but found it difficult to focus.

The dogs arrived demanding her attention and, more importantly, food. As she stood up to attend to them, it was as if a veil had been removed from her foggy brain, and she shouted out, 'They didn't travel by plane! That was a ruse; a red herring to confuse the airport authorities! So, where did they go and how did they travel?'

Curley and Topsy, catching her enthusiasm, jumped and ran around their owner, believing themselves to be the cause of her elation.

'Now, where could they have gone?' She quickly Googled transport from Bathurst to... Where? Her mind was overloaded with confused ideas. She contacted Maggie to brainstorm her thoughts.

'Mags, my mind is in overdrive. Those kids have pulled the wool over our eyes and have gone off by other means of transport. We need to contact Jett to find out ways of travelling on from there.'

'Julie, slow down and catch your breath,' Maggie laughed at her friend's excitement. 'You won't ever let go of a thought, will you, until you have seen it through? Look, I was planning to call Hermione in a day or two, but I'll call earlier and run this past them. Jonny is due home tomorrow and no doubt he will be pleased to catch up with you.'

The two talked for some time until Julie, aware of the dogs trying to get her attention and realising that she had omitted to feed them, ended the conversation with a promise to be keep in touch.

∞

Investigation continued to locate the two suspects. It appeared that no record was found of either a Max or Val García arriving or leaving Australian shores. Their names were flagged, Googled, and checked at all Australian airports, but to no avail. It seemed that they had simply vanished. Detectives in charge of the case looked to the Fraud Squad to assist them.

'No-one can enter Australia without a valid passport, so we are now looking at forged passports and visas,' commented an official from the Australia Border Force. They patrol airports and seaports, and work closely with other law enforcements and government agencies to protect the country from terrorists, organised crime gangs, and such like.

'It is possible that these two passengers managed to slip through without proper checks being made,' commented a senior officer. 'Unusual, but not outwith the realms of possibility, if the documents looked professional and did not flag up any concern.'

In case the suspects had travelled by sea, ship passenger names were scrutinised and compared to the grainy pictures that Chester had downloaded from the CCTV monitor at Bathurst Airport. An officer from the squad assigned to scrutinise documents suggested that perhaps the couple had not travelled together and had in fact entered the country separately.

'So, let's look for solo travellers. Start the search again,' he sighed.

∞

Several miles from Chestermere Hall, in a rundown area of a large industrial town, a fraught conversation had taken place.

'Da, don't make me do this. Da, I'm scared. I hate flying and I don't know the guy Frankie you're talking about. I'm not going to Australia with him.'

'Listen here to me, girl. You've got a chance in a million to see another part of the world. Kids your age would give their right arm for a trip like this. Frankie's okay, he was my best mate for years in jail. All you need to do is follow his instructions and keep your mouth shut. He's doing a job for me and you're needed to make things respectable. What better cover than a couple of students on a gap year?'

'A year?' yelled Zara. 'I ain't going anywhere for a year.'

'Calm down, kid. That's the cover story, that you and Frankie are students. You'll only be there a couple of weeks at the most, quick in and out and get the job done,'

'What job? What are you making me do, Da?'

'Everything will be made clear later. You don't have to do anything, just be there with Frankie.'

Zara cried herself to sleep that night. Her sleep was disturbed by thoughts of planes crashing into each other and her being abducted by strange men in prison garb. She had no-one to turn to. Her alcoholic mother had been out of her life for several years. Zara lived, or rather existed, with her overbearing father who, on release from prison, had claimed her from the foster home where she'd led an idyllic life for three years. Her maternal grandparents fought for custody of her, but due to their advancing age and ill health, the court rejected their request. Zara found it hard to adjust to living with her sole parent. With little support or understanding from him, she had begun to self-harm and sink into depression. Unable to hold down any employment, she kept house for her father who had succeeded in gaining employment as a security officer at a local airport. His hours were long and spasmodic, leaving Zara to her own devices. Her existence was at best lonely, and at worst miserable.

He sat with his distressed daughter, unable to understand her fear.

'Zara, I've got two cheap tickets through my work, and paid all taxes and airport fees. You're going with Frankie and no arguments. We've got to get the job done.'

'Da, what's the job? You haven't told me anything about it.'

'Frankie is going to retrieve some rare jewels and different kinds of precious items. Zara, lass, it's going to change our lives. Just think, you can have all the pretty things you've ever wanted, and we can move from this hovel to a better area.'

'What do you mean... retrieve? Where is he going to get these things from? Da, what's going on?'

'Kid, don't worry. Everything is planned. Frankie will open a safe, take the stuff, and you'll both come back with the goodies. Frankie is a good guy; the best safe-breaker since Johnny Ramensky.'

'Who?'

'Before your time. Johnny Ramensky was the best safe-blower of all time. He spent most of his life in and out of prison, until the government released him during the war to work for them by blowing safes to get information on the enemy.'

Zara was stunned. 'You're sending me across the world to steal? Da, that's the worst thing you've ever done. No, I'm not going. Can he not just open a safe nearer home? Why does it have to be Australia? I'm not going.'

There was a sharp crack and her head spun from the slap on her cheek. She stood to run to her room but was restrained by a firm grasp of her arm.

'You're gonna do what I ask,' snapped her father. 'Everything is arranged, there's no going back. So, get real and get packing. I'm taking you to Spain to meet Frankie – that's where he lives. There's lots to sort out like passports, new names for you both, and plans to make.'

He adopted a cajoling tone. 'Don't be scared, kid, I'm sorry I hit you. Didn't mean that to happen. You'll be fine with Frankie, just do what he asks and keep your mouth shut. You'll go as brother and sister, living and studying in Spain, so we need you to develop a bit of an accent. We'll work out the details when we get to Madrid. I'm taking you there to hook up with your new brother.'

Zara was distraught.

Within a week, with her father holding firmly onto her arm should she attempt to run from him, she boarded a flight to Madrid. Her father had given her some sleeping pills, so she fastened her seatbelt, faced the window and slept the entire flight.

On arrival, she felt woozy and was content to hold her father's arm as he led her to meet the mysterious Frankie. They took a local taxi to a beach area some miles from the airport, where Frankie managed a thriving bar and ran it with precision. He lived in a flat above the pub, and the trio met there to discuss the Australian trip.

Zara was pleasantly surprised at how amicable and welcoming her travel companion was. Her initial terror subsided as she listened to the plans for the trip.

'First things first, Zara,' Frankie told her. 'We have new passports, so hide the legal one you came over here with. You'll need it to get back home from Spain. You are now Val García, and I'm your older and wiser brother, Max.' He smiled kindly at her. 'So, we practise calling each other by those names, starting now.'

Frankie was heavily built – not tall, but with a wide grin and affable nature. His ginger hair flopped over his face as he spoke, and he habitually pushed it from his forehead. He was not what Zara had imagined an ex-con to be; that role of thuggish convict belonged to her father. She wondered how the men had influenced each other during their time in prison.

Frankie was calm and totally in control as he explained his past life to her.

'I'm not a bad person, Zara... sorry, Val. I'm not a thug, just an ordinary guy who has a knack of opening safes and got a bit blasé and careless and got caught. I've done a few jobs, mainly easy stuff, but this Australian job is right up my street.'

Zara looked pleadingly at her father who was watching her reaction to everything that was being said.

'Zara, we can't let a chance like this go by,' he said. 'We've got to make a move. I inspected the most incredible collection of jewellery, rings, brooches, necklaces, diamonds galore that a couple of stupid women were taking to Australia, I have all the details of where they are. I've never seen such a collection, ever. They're on a ranch-place, that's where you're going, to work there... supposedly. I'm sure the stuff won't be lying around. It will be stored somewhere like a safe, and Frankie will suss the place out to find the safe.'

'But why do you need me there, Da?' she whined. 'Can't Frankie manage on his own? I'm scared to go all that way. I hate flying.'

'Kid, you did fine on the flight over here now, didn't you? There's nought to fear. Your old da wouldn't put you in any danger, would he?'

Zara had an answer to that but kept her thoughts to herself. She knew her ruthless father would sacrifice anyone who thwarted his plans.

Frankie, now Max, interrupted. 'Val, it will be the easiest thing in the world. You won't have to do a thing except maybe be a look-out for me. We'll have a good time on the ranch-place helping with the animals and easy stuff.'

Her heart dropped again. 'I'm scared of animals,' she admitted. 'I don't much like them.'

Her father was struggling to control his temper. 'I didn't raise you to be a wimp,' he snapped. 'Listen to Max, he'll look after you.'

Max continued, 'We'll go as brother and sister. The cover is you're waiting to be given a place at college to learn Spanish cooking so that you can help me in the bar. I'll invent a college course for myself, should anyone ask, and I know enough of the language now to get by. I'll teach you a few phrases and we'll work on getting rid of your accent, just in case we meet up with any Spaniards over there.'

Zara felt reasonably comfortable with her new companion, and relaxed as they shared a meal at his downstairs bar.

'Oh, another thing,' he said. 'As we're supposed to be poor students, we'll be sharing a room in one of the bedsits on the ranch. Single beds, of course.'

Zara looked horrified at the thought but was quickly put at ease when he declared that he had no interest in women and that she would have all the privacy she needed. Zara had not realised until then that Frankie was gay.

With everything in place and forged documents in their possession, the adventurers set off. Frankie had been given some pills from Val's father with instructions to *feed them to her, and she'll sleep most of the journey.*

While she slept, waking only to eat, Max enjoyed the on-board film and relaxed for the first time in many months. Despite his past, he was a hard worker and had turned the bar into a viable business.

As they disembarked at Sydney Airport, he was a tad anxious as to how they would pull off the use of forged passports. He held Val firmly by his side as they walked towards Customs and Passport Control. A troublesome passenger was causing mayhem, and arriving travellers were herded quickly through by authorities. Max and Val's passports were given a cursory glance by an official who was called to help with the disruptive passenger.

'Move along quickly, keep to the left,' he called to the crowd.

∞

Unlike Julie and Maggie, Zara had not been afforded the luxury of a stop-over and was completely exhausted and nervous by the time she arrived at the homestead. Onward travel from Sydney had been torturous for a fraught girl who had never before travelled more than a few miles from her home. The vastness of the homestead frightened her, as did the sight of so many raucous ranchers whose welcoming *G'day* in a strange accent unsettled her.

She now felt comfortable in Max's company but was keen not to make mistakes and disappoint him. They had slipped easily into the habit of referring to each other by their new names, but she hated meeting new people and was over-awed by the size of the place. Terrified of becoming lost, she stuck close to Max.

When he was helping on the ranch, she spent time on her own in her room or helped house staff with some chores. As their stay progressed, she found herself enjoying Max's company and listened with some admiration to his tales of bravado in his youth. She found him easy to talk to and off-loaded her feelings about her father and her hatred of the mother who had abandoned her.

Max spoke about her father and the time they spent together in prison. 'I didn't particularly like him,' he admitted, 'but had to get on with him as we were sharing a cell for what seemed like an eternity. He was a rough character and got into fights with anyone who looked sideways at him. I was grateful in a way to have him at my side, though, as gay guys can have it rough in prison.'

He chuckled as he continued, 'No-one would annoy me knowing he was my protector, so I'm not surprised that you are afraid of him. I hated the guy, but then he called and told me about the jewels and stuff, where they were heading, and offered to pay me to go get them. I thought, why the heck not? Then he came up with the idea of you coming along as a kind of cover for us being backpacking students.'

He shrugged. 'I was reluctant at first but fell in with his plan. He offered a free trip to Australia, so I didn't question where the money came from to pay for it. Reece had his own way of getting dosh and I had a healthy bank balance, so, hey, I said, go for it.'

Val also wondered where her father's money had come from. They lived in poverty, with few home comforts, and he gave her a pittance for housekeeping. She knew, though, that he had been imprisoned for his part in a shop raid where thousands of pounds had been stolen and never recovered.

Max interrupted her thoughts to explain his plan.

'I have to get into the main house and locate the safe,' he said, 'that's my first task, then I'll think of a way of opening it when there's no-one around.'

He laughed and continued, 'There hasn't been a safe that's beaten me yet. In jail, they called me the Piggy-Bank-Kid; they knew I could open any safe, anywhere. I'm keeping my eyes open as to when the main house is likely to be empty, and that's when you need to be my look-out. It seems like there's a quiet spell after lunch when everyone has gone back to work. This is where you come in. You stay by the door and alert me if anyone comes by. That's all you have to do, be eyes and ears for me.'

∞

They settled into a routine, with Max enjoying the challenge of working with the stockmen and Val staying around the compound helping with some chores. She spoke little, her fear of revealing too much information foremost in her thoughts. Shazzie, the senior housekeeper, had taken her under her wing, and showed her where Hermione left the cleaning items up at the main house. The door was unlocked, which Shazzie explained was the norm.

'We're all trusted to respect things around here,' Shazzie told her. 'Hermione and Jett want folks to be able to pop in for cold drinks when they are passing by. They trust us to be honest, and people appreciate it. In all my years here, we've never had any trouble with thieving and the like.'

'Have you lived here long?' the shy girl enquired.

Shazzie smiled. 'All my life, actually. I was born on the compound. My mother was involved with one of the guys – a clandestine affair, she told me. He, my father, was bit of a lad and had several affairs... and a wife.'

Shazzie giggled as she related the tale of her wayward father.

'My mother died several years ago. She fell from a horse that got spooked when they were caught in a thunderstorm.'

As she spoke, the older woman opened a heart-shaped locket that hung around her neck. 'That's my mother. Madeleine, they called her Maddie, for short.'

Val struggled with her emotions. 'She looks beautiful,' she said quietly. 'I wish my mam was like her. She took off when I was a baby, because she couldn't cope with a screaming child. I don't know if she is dead or alive.'

Shazzie gave Val a comforting hug as she closed the locket.

'Right,' she said with a smile, 'here's the stuff we need. You take this bundle and I'll get the rest.'

As they left the kitchen area, Val spotted a built-in safe on the far wall.

Max was delighted with her observation as it helped to move him a step forward to his goal.

'Good for you, Val, that's exactly what I need from you. I'll figure out how to get the stuff out of the safe then we can plan for home.'

The next few days were busy for the two farm-stay visitors, as a new group of holiday workers had arrived, and bunkhouses and rooms needed to be made ready. Once again, Val found herself in the kitchen area to collect some items. Knowing she was alone, she took a picture on her phone that gave Max information on the make and model of the safe.

Max laughed as he studied the photo later. 'If I didn't know you better,' he said, 'I'd say you were enjoying this cloak and dagger stuff.'

She smiled, unused to using her facial muscles. 'Funnily enough, I am enjoying being a bit of a detective,' she admitted. 'I haven't had such excitement in a while, but I'm scared of stealing the stuff from the safe and getting caught.'

Max shook his head. 'Don't concern yourself about that. I'll be doing the donkey work, you just keep doing what you're doing and keep your eyes and ears open. I overheard one of the guys – Smokey, they call him – saying he was taking two visitors out riding on Monday. They're the Brits that seem to be relatives of the owners and live in the main house. So, if they are out the path should be clear for me to pop in and check the safe. Jett is always out early on the station.'

'What about the boss woman, Hermione, where does she go during the day?' asked Val, whose anxiety was returning at the thought of the impending theft.

'Leave that to me. If she's in the house, I'll find a way of getting her out.

'You won't harm her, will you?'

'No, there will be no violence. Now help me gather some small stones. I've a plan to put in place.'

∞

After parking the truck belonging to the ranch, and leaving the keys inside, Max led Val through the airport concourse towards the exit near the road transport hub.

'Keep your head down, don't look at anyone, and keep moving. We'll be out of here soon. Pretend we're searching for our flight.'

Val did as bid, more from fear than anything else. She kept close to Max; she was scared of losing him in the melee of airport activity.

Outside in the truckers' area, Max searched for means of catching a ride away from the area as quickly as possible, and hopefully before their absence and that of the missing pickup truck was noticed.

After half an hour with no luck, they went to sit in the café area. Max devoured his food while Val toyed with hers.

'Val, eat up, kid,' he urged. 'It might be some time before we have another meal.'

'I'm too nervous to eat,' she whispered. 'What's happening? I'm scared, Max.'

'Trust me. I'll get us a ride out of here before we're missed, and make our way homeward bound. But it's going to take days, so don't expect to be home any time soon.'

Just then, he noticed a trucker finishing his meal and heading out to his vehicle.

'Stay here, Val,' said Max. 'I'll be back in a minute.'

He caught up with the driver outside. 'Excuse me, sir, any chance of a ride for me and my sister? We'd sure appreciate it.'

'I've got a long haul ahead, kid. Heading to the Melbourne area, but stopping at Beechworth where my shift finishes,' the driver told him. 'You're welcome to tag along as far as there, but I have to warn you it will take about six hours.'

Max grinned. 'That would be great, thanks. I'll fetch my sister and visit the bathroom first. Much appreciated. I'm Max, by the way, and my kid sister is Val.'

'Steve.' The driver nodded. 'Steve Morrow, pleased to have you on board and glad of the company. It can be a long lonely ride at times.'

Max fetched Val and scooped the remains of their meal into a take-out box. 'Leave me to do the talking,' he told her. 'I'll think of a cover story. Don't let out that we've been on a ranch. Let's get going.'

Introductions over, and with Val sitting behind her brother to allow her some space, they set off. After some chit-chat, Steve noticed his passengers were fighting sleep and suggested they rested. He turned the radio on and sang softly to the music. He drove steadily along the Hume highway and made good time to Beechworth where he parted company with his passengers, but not before directing them to a hostel where they could find accommodation and spend the night.

'Good to have you on board, safe onward travel,' he told them. 'You kids take care of each other.'

∞

'I'm exhausted, Max. I can't sleep properly, I keep having scary dreams. Where are we and where are we going now?' asked Val, when they left the hostel after a restless night.

She'd had to share a dorm with three other females and had been scared for her life when they began drinking and sharing drugs. She'd feigned sleep to avoid becoming involved.

'I'm checking this timetable,' Max replied. 'We'll catch a bus to Melbourne, the next one leaves in an hour. So, we've time to pick up some food for the journey. It takes about three hours, according to this guide.'

'All you think of is food,' grumbled Val, who was as nervous now as she had been before leaving home to begin their epic journey. 'I can't take all this travel.'

'Val, we want to get as far away as possible and head for home. Don't you want to go home?'

At the mention of home, she fought back tears. She wasn't missing her father at all but was resigned to what lay ahead.

The three-hour journey passed quickly for them. Val, emotionally exhausted, slept the entire time with her head on Max's shoulder. He was wide awake. Having worked out a plan for ongoing travel, he was preparing himself for her reaction when he shared his thoughts. *It's for the best,* he told himself. *But how do I convince Val without her going into meltdown?*

∞

'Val, this is what I've come up with. This is where we split company and go our separate ways. It's for the best.'

Max put a protective arm around the terrified girl as he explained his plan to get her home safely to Britain.

'I'll book you on a flight home. It's non-stop, takes hours and hours, so you won't have to worry about stop-overs,' he said. 'Watch the onboard films, eat when they bring you food, and read a magazine. Sleep when you can. The time will pass quickly enough, and you'll be on home soil before you know it.

'Use your legal passport and become Zara Davies again. You'll have nothing to worry about, just say you've been visiting relatives, should anyone ask. We'll pick up a puzzle book to help pass the time. I'll text your dad with flight times and he'll be sure to meet you and take you home.' He hugged her close. 'Things are going to be fine, kid.'

Feeling panicky, she shook uncontrollably.

'I hate flying, Max,' she moaned, 'I just hate it. I'll be scared on my own. Why can't we travel together?'

He took a deep breath. 'Kid, I'll be going to Spain, back to my work in the bar, but I'm taking a long-convoluted route to avoid detection. It's safer for us both to travel separately. I'd worry about the authorities looking for us as a couple. You'll be home long before me. Don't fret.'

The duo hung around Melbourne long enough for Max to organise a flight ticket and for the now Zara to calm down and accept her fate.

'Okay, kid, here's your ticket and flight details,' he told her. 'I'll go with you through check-in and walk along with you as far as I'm allowed, then you follow the path to the departure gate. The number is on your ticket. Listen out for your flight to be called and follow the other passengers. Kid, you'll be fine.'

Zara held onto him and sobbed quietly. She knew his plan was in her best interests, but she was still nervous.

'You've been good to me,' she cried, 'the only friend I've ever had. I'll miss you.'

Max, knowing that he had done all he could to assure Zara's safe return to UK, accompanied her as far as the departure area, where he gave her a reassuring hug and peck on the cheek.

'You'll be fine, don't worry.' He smiled encouragingly. 'Look, follow that family, they're booked on your flight. Keep them in sight. You'll be fine, kid.'

Once she was out of sight, he headed off to plan his own return to Spain. He holed up in a cheap hostel, checked the internet for ways and means to travel home, then began a painstaking journey involving bus, train, and truck journeys.

∞

Jack Adamson, excitement evident in his voice, contacted Jonny to update him on the results of forensic testing on the comb which Julie had retrieved.

'We have a match, Jonny! Your writer friend has come up trumps by finding that comb,' he explained. 'We have made a connection with a known British criminal – one Frank Preston, a well-known safe-breaker who spent time in prison, was released on parole, and vanished from the face of the earth. Detectives suspected he had gone to ground, as there's been no trace of him until now.

'Looks like your thief was working and living on your sister's ranch. The Australian cops are onto him, but, hey, we've cracked it. The other DNA result is that of a female – a British citizen, Zara Davies. She doesn't appear to have a criminal past but was traced via social works records. Seems she was an abused kid and was in foster care for a time while her criminal father served time for violence. There was a court custody case. Her grandparents wanted to have her live with them, but they lost the case due to their advancing age and ill health. Those two could well be the Val and Max who've taken off with the jewels. Lyndon Craig, the Aussie scientist, has completed testing on the items he holds over there and has confirmed our findings.'

Jonny was ecstatic as he related the news to first his wife, and then Hermione.

'Oh, I must give Julie a call this evening,' said an excited Maggie. 'She will be delighted to hear that her detective's gut feeling about Max and Val was right all along. Why did I ever doubt her?'

Several more calls were made back and forth between UK and Australian detectives and scientists, and alerts were put out for both Zara Davies and Frank Preston, aka Val and Max García. Prison records were checked and revealed that Frank Preston and Reece Davies, Zara's father, shared a cell for three years while serving time. Frank Preston, a model prisoner in the eyes of the wardens, was granted time out of prison on parole but failed to return to jail. Instead, he had travelled to Spain within hours of release, and was sunning himself at a beach bar before his due time to return to prison was up.

Things were falling into place. But where were the two thieves now?

∞

Zara Davies, unaware of the search for her, settled to a comfortable flight home. She was seated beside a motherly lady who was travelling to London to visit her sister whom she hadn't seen for ten years. She was an interesting woman who was so caught up in the excitement of meeting her relative that she didn't pry into Zara's life at all.

'My kid sister is eight years younger than me,' she said, as she produced a picture of a portly version of the slim lady sitting beside Zara. 'That's my Eleanor-Ann, the baby of the family. She met her husband, Wallace Grayson, in London when he was a guest in the hotel where she was a receptionist. He swept her off her feet; they got married in Marylebone Town Hall with my parents and myself as witnesses. Here's a picture of her in her wedding outfit. Isn't she stunning?'

Zara would have commented on the beautiful outfit if Jilly, as she discovered was her travelling companion's name, stopped long enough for breath. She regaled Zara with their plans to tour Britain until eventually she succumbed to sleep, leaving Zara free to plan her own life. She felt remarkably calm as she mulled over past events and planned how she was going to be stronger and stand up to her father's bullying.

With positive thoughts coursing through her, she gave into sleep, her mind clearing of hurtful memories. *I won't go back to live with him. I'll declare myself homeless and take every ounce of help that will turn my life around. I might move to the coast...* she thought, oblivious to what lay ahead to thwart her plans. As she travelled back to the UK, she was unaware that the authorities had been alerted to search for her and that her name had been flagged up after her flight had taken off.

The passenger in question is on board flight 406 seated in row 14d. The crew has been alerted and will discreetly observe the passenger,' was the message from the officer in charge of airport procedure. *'She will disembark with the rest of the passengers and will be apprehended in the Customs Hall.*

∞

Frank Preston, aka Max García, did not fare quite as well as planned. Having seen Zara off and texted her father her arrival time, he boarded a bus that would take him to Melbourne. The twelve-hour journey was comfortable for the fugitive, with reclining seats and no-one seated nearby to become involved in idle chat with. He had hoped to board a freight ship at Freemantle as a foot passenger, but freight ships, he was to discover, were few and far between.

By now, his cash flow from his legit bar business and the dollars he had been given for Zara's needs, were slowly dwindling. The cheapest flight home was beyond his means as he had spent most of the cash to secure a non-stop flight for Zara.

He needed a plan. He needed a job. One of the harbour pubs required staff, so he worked tirelessly there as Max García for several weeks. For a few dollars, the owner lent him a spare room above the pub. The man was pleased with his latest recruit, as most of his employees could not handle the long hours and physical work involved in moving heavy beer barrels.

As the weeks went by, he came to entrust the young Englishman with more responsibility, including cashing up and storing the day's takings in the pub safe. This Max did diligently, while all the time planning his journey home. Armed with all the information he required, he waited for an opportune moment to put his plan into action.

As the time approached for a ferry to sail to downtown Perth, Max took his chance when the bar was quiet. The only two customers, seated out of view of the bar area, were engrossed in the latest rugby news and were unaware of the barman's activities. Clay Roache, the owner, was working in the cellar.

Max took the opportunity to grab and go. He pocketed as many dollars as he could, grabbed his bag which was under the counter, and fled to B Shed at Victoria Quay. His timing was perfect. No sooner had he purchased a forty-dollar ticket and boarded the ferry, than it set sail on the thirty-minute journey that was to take him a step nearer home.

His sigh of relief was to be short-lived.

∞

The aircraft carrying the now refreshed Zara Davies touched down like a bird landing carefully on its personal spot. Once the seatbelt sign went off, passengers gathered their belongings, then headed out of the aircraft. Jilly gave her young companion a hug and thanked her for her company.

'I so enjoyed chatting to you. It helped pass the time, my dear. Take care of yourself. I must rush. Eleanor-Ann will be waiting for me.'

Zara smiled, knowing that she had hardly spoken more than a few sentences to the excited lady. She collected her one piece of luggage from the carousel and followed the crowd to Passport Control, where an official checked her document and said, 'Welcome back to the UK, ma'am.'

Unknown to Zara, he had pressed an alert button on his desk. As she headed to the Customs area and was about to walk through, an official stopped her in her tracks. 'Madam, please follow me to this area for a bag check. Just routine, madam.' Being aware of airport security, Zara did as bid and placed her bag on the desk. She was asked routine questions about who had packed the bag, did it belong to her, and where she had travelled from. She answered calmly and clearly, not feeling threatened in any way.

At that point, two more officials approached. 'Ma'am, please follow us to this private room,' said one. 'We have a few more questions to ask.'

The room was sparsely furnished with three chairs and a table, on which sat a recording device. For what seemed an endless time, the officers perused her passport while she sat quietly. As if a light had suddenly been switched on, it dawned on Zara that there was more to this routine questioning than she'd first thought, and she became nervous.

Her brow trickled with sweat, her hands were clammy, her mouth felt like sandpaper. She wiped her brow with a handkerchief and wriggled in her seat.

'Are you alright, Ms Davies? Can we get you some water?' asked the female official while the older, male officer stared at Zara in a manner that made her even more uncomfortable.

It took all Zara's strength to reply with the affirmative.

The officials switched on the recorder and introduced themselves, 'Present at this interview on September 21st at 08:15 is Officer Mark James, Officer Cheryl Munro and passenger Zara Davies.' He detailed other information before turning to Zara.

'Please confirm your name for the purpose of this interview.'

He spoke curtly and loudly, which only added to Zara's anxiety.

'Your date of birth? Your UK address? Next of kin?'

As he wrote furiously, his colleague, Officer Munro, questioned Zara as to her reason for visiting Australia... who she'd travelled with... how long she had stayed there... and where she had stayed. The continual questioning made her flustered and tongue-tied. Frankie had not prepared her for the possibility of such intrusive questions.

Her heart seemed as if it were going to burst, and her voice faltered as she stuttered her replies to the questions that seemed to ricochet from Officer Munro. She bit her nails nervously and by sheer willpower, held back tears.

'You say you travelled with your brother? What is his name, please?'

'Max García' she replied, before realising her *faux pas*.

'Mm, he is your brother? Can you explain the difference in surnames?'

'I made a mistake. He's just a friend.'

'Is he a friend *or* is he your brother?'

'Just a friend.'

'And where is this friend now, Ms Davies?'

'I don't know. He's still in Australia, touring the country.'

The officers looked at each other before Officer James

spoke sternly and reduced her to tears with more rapid questioning.

'Tell me the name of your travelling companion. Please don't try to lie your way out of this,' he badgered her. 'You are hiding something, aren't you, Ms Davies? Let's begin with the truth.'

'Who did you travel to Australia with?' asked Officer Munro.

'Frankie Preston,' whispered Zara.

'Please repeat that louder for the purpose of the recording.'

It took all of her effort to raise her voice as she stumbled over his name.

Officer Munro took over the questioning as she handed Zara a dry tissue.

'Where did you first meet Frankie Preston?' she asked.

'In Spain.'

'Explain how that came about.'

'My da took me to Spain to meet him.'

Zara was ready to collapse with nervous exhaustion. Taking in her pale face and rapid breathing, the two officers became concerned about the state of her emotional health and decided to end the interview.

'Ms Davies,' said Officer Munro, a little kindlier. 'We have many questions to ask but we need the airport medic to examine you. Do you agree to that?'

Zara nodded her consent. By that stage she just wanted to lie down and weep for her foolishness at not standing up to her father and refusing to go with Frankie Preston on what was turning into a disastrous mission. She wondered where Frankie was now.

∞

Clay Roache clenched his fist and thumped it on the counter, rage flowing through him like a torrent of murky water on discovering that he had been duped into trusting his latest employee and that his week's takings had been stolen. He contacted the police, who tried to calm down the raging owner as he paced the floor like a demented animal, shouting obscenities at the top of his voice.

'To think that I trusted the sonofabitch. I took him in, gave him a roof over his head, and trusted my gut instinct that this was a good, casual worker, an honest man,' he complained. 'What a fool he's taken me for. He'll be laughing all the way to wherever the goddam man has gone.'

'Calm down, Mr. Roache,' soothed one of the police officers. 'We need you to calm down and give us a description of the guy you say stole your money.'

'I can do better than that,' he snapped. 'The CCTV will show the bar area. I switch it on at weekends and busy times when things get loud and punters get a bit wild. He should show up right here, working behind the bar. And to think I trusted that—'

'Okay, Mr Roache, let's have a look at the pictures.'

They scrolled through the footage as the camera swept across the bar to the seating area and back and halted when a barman was spotted clearing and wiping one of the tables.

'There he is, there's that scumbag who stole my money. Look at him, not a care in the world,' hollered Clay Roache, once more thumping his fist on the counter. 'That's him. That's Max García, that's the guy I trusted.'

'We'll scroll this film on a bit if you don't mind,' said the officer. 'It might show some more.'

As they watched in amazement, Max García was clearly seen crouching down behind the counter, opening the safe and filling a bag with notes.

'The drongo... the fool... idiot... the ratbag... he's made a fool of me!'

Clay Roache was incensed.

'No worries, sir,' the officer assured him, 'the guy's gone walkabout and we'll get him for sure.'

As he spoke, his colleague had called in the information to HQ and transferred images from the CCTV. Within minutes, he received a reply that the man known to the bar owner as Max García, was in fact Frank Preston – a known UK safe-breaker, wanted for absconding from prison, and remaining to this day unlawfully at large. He had failed to comply with his licence conditions and had dodged capture for six years. Now he was also a suspect in a robbery at a homestead outside Bathurst.

The officer related the information to the irate owner and assured him that the authorities were a step nearer to apprehending the criminal.

'I hope I get my money back,' Clay Roache spat out the words as he locked up his premises.

∞

Medical personnel examined Zara Davies and declared her fit for questioning. Meanwhile, an impatient Reece Davies paced the arrival terminal, craning his neck each time the door opened, impatient to collect his daughter and drive home. Eventually, when she still hadn't appeared, he headed to the customer service desk and joined a queue of people anxiously trying to obtain flight information.

'Excuse me,' he shouted rudely above the queue of people. 'My daughter arrived on flight 406 over an hour ago. Any idea where she is? I can't hang around here all day.'

One lady in the queue whispered to her companion, 'How rude. Some people have no manners and no patience.'

'Please wait, sir, while I deal with these people,' said the receptionist.

He muttered under his breath but had no choice other than to wait his turn.

'The flight has landed, sir,' the receptionist informed him once she took a note of the details. 'If you could take a seat over there, I'll call through to Customs to find out what the delay is. It gets very busy at times in the Customs Hall, especially when several flights arrive at once.'

The alert receptionist had noticed the name Zara Davies on her screen with a message to call security should she be seen anywhere in the airport concourse. She flagged up the details given by the impatient man, and discreetly pressed an alert button under her desk. Within minutes, two security officials approached Reece Davies with a request to follow them to a secure area.

'What's the fuck up? I've been here over an hour,' he stormed. 'This hanging about is costing me a fortune in parking charges. Where's my stupid daughter?'

'Mind your language, sir,' one of the officers told him sternly. 'We're in a public area. Seems like your daughter has taken ill and has to be checked by medics. Please come with us.'

They led him to a room off the Customs Hall and asked him to wait.

'Someone will be along soon, sir,' said one of the men.

Reece Davies fumed as he paced up and down the tiny room, his anger increasing by the minute. Unknown to him, an officer was outside the room, guarding the door should he attempt to leave. *What's the silly fool done now?* He grumbled to himself. *Can't she get herself off a plane without drawing attention to herself? When I get her home, I'll teach her not to keep me waiting.*

Zara Davies found herself back in the interview room with Officers Munro and James, having been declared fit to be interviewed. The recording procedure ready, the officers wasted no time in launching into question after question, giving her little time to think up an answer.

'Tell us what transpired in Spain, Ms Davies.'

'I've already told you,' replied Zara with a bravado she didn't know she possessed. 'My da took me to meet Frankie.'

'For what purpose?'

'To meet him before we flew to Australia.'

'Are you saying you had never met this Frankie character before then, and you were planning to fly to the other end of the world with him?'

Her voice faltered as she replied, 'I didn't plan anything, my da planned it all.'

The officers looked at each other before continuing. 'What was the purpose of the trip to Australia?'

'To see the country and do a bit of work on a big ranch.'

Officer Munro softened her voice to a less threatening level. 'Zara,' she said, 'things are not looking good for you. You had better tell us the entire truth about your trip, starting from the beginning. It won't do you any good if you conceal things from us. Start with your father... his name?'

'Reece Davies.' She spat his name out like a bad taste in her mouth. 'He's a beast, a monster, he rapes me every chance he gets, and locks me up. And I have to do what he tells me, or he batters me.'

Finally blurting out the truth, Zara burst into uncontrollable tears that had been suppressed for so long. The officers let her weep until she had no more tears to shed. Officer James quietly left the room to contact his superior.

∞

Officer Munro led the distraught girl to a more comfortable room where she could speak calmly to her. With gentle and sympathetic probing, she elicited the truth from the shaken girl as she off-loaded her tragic life story, like peeling an onion until there was nothing left to tell.

'Oh, you poor dear!' Tracey Munro was not the fierce, unsmiling official she portrayed to the public. She had a heart of gold and felt immensely sorry for the young woman who had unburdened her feelings to her.

'I'm never going back to him, ever,' cried Zara. 'I'll kill myself if I have to live with him again.'

'No need to worry on that score, Zara,' Officer Munro assured her. 'I don't think you'll be seeing him for a long time. Once we arrest him and press charges, he'll be in prison for a long stretch.'

She did not tell Zara that she could well be returned to Australia to face charges for being an accessory to a crime – a charge that carried a minimum jail sentence of five years.

The airport officials fast-tracked the case of Zara Davies, and she was removed to a place of safety where social workers detailed her horrendous life and checked files from her earlier time in their care.

A senior care worker told her team, 'This kid was removed from the family home when she was eight years of age, when her father was sentenced to three years for assault and battery after a pub brawl. He had a criminal record as long as your arm, including armed robbery from a shop. The mother, a known alcoholic, had taken off some years previously and was found drowned in the river.

'I believe Zara was never given that information and may still not be aware that her mother died. The girl was placed with a foster family for the duration of her father's imprisonment and thrived in their care. On Reece Davies' release from prison, he fought to have his daughter – now almost twelve years old – handed back into his care.

'The vulnerable girl was monitored for a time by our department. Home visits were made, and all seemed in order. The father was charming, the girl understandably shy, but she assured staff that she was happy to be home. Her school, however, reported a different story: she was unkempt, always hungry, and fell way behind with school work. She had no friends and would not open up to counselling staff at school.

'Several home visits were made until Madge Ramsey, her care worker, retired. The file was handed over to be followed up, but for some reason, when a young, inexperienced care worker, believing that all was well, discharged the girl from our system.'

'What happens now to the girl, or should I say young woman?' asked a team member.

'The Australian court wants an in-depth background report on her before deciding whether to proceed with criminal charges. I've been given the task of co-ordinating a social work report, and all of you,' she pointed to her team, 'will be allocated an area of her life to investigate: Alan, you will investigate Reece Davies; Jackie, you're in charge of finding out all you can about the mother, Rachel Davies; Tommy, you take on the task of locating and speaking to the foster parents, Irene and Robin McLaren; Martin, your task is to locate school reports.

'We also need to investigate the influence Frank Preston had on the girl. Angela, that is your remit; and Larry, you get onto the Australian owners of the ranch where she stayed and get their take on her. Any problems, get back to me ASAP. Meanwhile, Zara Davies is being counselled and cared for in a secure unit with round the clock surveillance, as she has mentioned several times that she wants to die. So far, she has been co-operative, but her emotional vulnerability is there for all to see. She is like a child in an adult body.'

∞

After thirty minutes waiting in the interview room with an officer outside the room, a furious Reece Davies began banging on the locked door.

'Let me out of this damn place. Where's my fucking daughter? Let me out, you idiot.' He felt as if he was once more in a prison interview room but was left to sweat it out until eventually two officers arrived.

'About time,' he snapped at them. 'What's going on? You can't keep me here. I've done nothing wrong except try to find my idiot of a daughter. Who's going to pay my parking fees? Where is she?'

'Sit down, sir,' commanded one of the officers, whose calm authority startled Reece Davies. He believed himself to be a law above everyone else and answerable to no-one, but this formidable officer scared him into submission. He perched on the edge of the chair and waited.

The officer continued, 'Reece Davies, you are under arrest for the statutory rape of a minor... You have the right to remain silent...'

As the officer continued to read him his Miranda rights, Davies was stunned into disbelief. Sweat poured from his brow as he stumbled against the table. He could hardly breathe, the room began to swim, and his head was filled with jumbled thoughts. He could barely think straight and mumbled an almost inaudible 'yes' when asked if he understood the charges.

He could not fathom how the authorities knew of his vile past. He had always been sure that his control over his daughter and her fear of him would keep his actions from ever being discovered. *If you ever tell anyone about this, I'll find you and kill you,* he had told the traumatised girl. And she had always complied. *I promise, Da,* she would reply. *I won't tell anyone. I love you, Da, please don't hurt me.*

Still reeling from the shock, he was led away to await his fate.

∞

Frank Preston, unaware of events in the UK and presuming Zara had arrived safely and been met by her father, stood on the deck of the ferry enjoying the sea breeze and planning his next move. He used his phone to investigate flights from Perth to Spain and discovered that there was a flight to Barcelona scheduled for later that day. He planned to pay by cash at the airport and be back where he called home before very long.

A perfect end to a perfect break. He smiled as he thought of the dollars and small jewellery pieces concealed in the false bottom of his case. *Too bad I was disturbed by that wretched woman calling out when I thought the house was empty, otherwise I'd have snaffled the lot.*

With his mind focused on his haul, he was oblivious to the presence of police officers waiting on the quayside as the ferry pulled into the harbour.

∞

Julie Sinclair sat with Maggie in Liz's sitting room while the latter fussed over preparing lunch. It wasn't often that the trio managed to spend time together, and they were determined to make the most of Maggie's short visit.

Julie called through to Liz, who was engrossed in putting the finishing touches to her home-made lasagne.

'Liz, we could have gone out for lunch to save you the trouble of cooking.'

'It's not a problem,' their friend called back. 'This way we can chill out and chat without disturbing others with our raucous laughter. Maggie, start pouring that lovely wine your darling Jonny sent. He knows us well – only the best will do.'

The women laughed as they enjoyed spending time together, reminiscing over their years of unbroken friendship which had only strengthened as the years went by. Talk eventually came around to the incident in Australia, and a sadness lingered as they shared the events and subsequent developments – a sadness for the life that Zara Davies had endured, and their inability to assist her.

'To think what that kid went through, living with that dreadful father,' said Maggie, 'it doesn't bear thinking about. If only she had confided in us, we could have done something to help her.'

'Yes,' said Julie, 'but she was under Max, sorry, Frank Preston's influence, and I'm sure she was afraid of him too. She was such a vulnerable young girl, and miles from her home country. Had they stayed around a bit longer, we might eventually have got her to confide in one of us.'

'What's happening to her now?' asked Liz.

Julie took up the story. 'The Australian authorities have not taken any action to call her back as yet. She pled guilty to being an accessory to the crime via video link, with her lawyer in attendance, I believe. And he told the court that in his opinion, his client was so damaged that he was unsure if she fully understood court procedure. It seems that the detailed report from social care people was favourably looked upon, and the authorities imposed a five-year suspended sentence, as long as she remains in social care. It appears that her mental health problems are such that she will live in a secure adult establishment, perhaps for the rest of her life.'

'What a brute of a father to destroy a life like that,' voiced Liz as she poured more wine for her friends. 'I hope he burns in hell.'

'He certainly won't see freedom for a long time,' said Maggie, 'if ever. Life for child abusers is not particularly comfortable in prison. Prisoners, for all their criminal activities, look very unfavourably on such people. Inmates have their own code of conduct. I imagine that Reece Davies will find that hell has visited him.'

'No wonder his wife left him. She must have gone through torture, too,' mused Julie as she sipped her wine. 'It seems like her mental health was such that she couldn't cope any longer. I suppose she could have taken her child with her, but if she planned to kill herself, she probably didn't have the nerve to kill her own child. Why, oh why didn't she go to the authorities? It would have saved young Zara from a life of hell. What a situation to be in, and all because of one vile man.'

Maggie added, 'And as for the Max fellow – I can't get used to calling him anything else – he was apprehended and arrested at Perth. He must have been mad to think he could smuggle the jewels through Customs when every suit-case is x-rayed.' She shook her head in disbelief. 'He faces a long term in prison. Thankfully, the various items were undamaged because he had wrapped them up carefully, and Hermione has had them returned to her. The end of a nasty episode.'

'All's well that ends well, as the esteemed Shakespeare said,' Liz commented, as she refilled the wine glasses.

Maggie smiled. 'And I have some good news. Bradley's wife, Milly, has given birth to a healthy baby girl. They are all besotted with her. Look, I have a few pictures on my phone.' She looked at Julie as she added, 'They have named her Julie-Margaret!'

'Oh!' Julie beamed in delight. 'What an honour to have a child named for you. She will have a special place in my heart.'

'Mine, too,' laughed Maggie. 'Bradley wanted to acknowl-edge your help in once again retrieving the items that meant so much to his mother, and Milly insisted my name be included, too. Isn't it wonderful? And Hermione has a special piece of jewellery put aside for her granddaughter when she is older.' 'What a story she will have to tell her! This calls for another bottle to be opened,' insisted Liz. 'We have to wet the baby's head with a toast to Julie-Margaret Lee.'

'I have other news, too,' grinned Maggie, her face flushed from a combination of wine and excitement, 'Hermione is coming over for two months later in the year, when Parliament is in recess and Jonny can spend time with his sister. Jett feels she has been through so much emotional upset that she needs a break. She will once more be in her family home at Chestermere Hall, and hopefully she will be able to lay a few ghosts to rest. You two are invited to stay for a while. It will be fun all being together again.'

'And noisy,' said the slightly merry Liz. 'Just think… a break for Julie has turned into a break for Hermione. Bring it on, girls. Cheers everyone! Cheers!'

THE END

ABOUT THE AUTHOR

Terry H Watson qualified in D.C.E. and Dip.Sp.Ed. from Notre Dame College, Glasgow and Bearsden, and obtained a B.A. degree from Open University Scotland.

A retired special needs teacher, Terry began writing in 2014 and has published a mystery thriller trilogy: THE LUCY TRILOGY: CALL MAMA; SCAMPER'S FIND; and THE LECI LEGACY.

She has written a compilation of short stories: A TALE OR TWO AND A FEW MORE, and a children's book: THE CLOCK THAT LOST ITS TICK AND OTHER TALES.

This latest publication – a cosy, mystery novella – is the second in the series, A JULIE SINCLAIR INVESTIGATES.

Terry welcomes reviews for her books.

You can contact her at
Twitter: https://twitter.com/terryhwatson1
e-mail: terryhwatson@yahoo.co.uk

Lightning Source UK Ltd.
Milton Keynes UK
UKHW021954061218
333582UK00003B/50/P